PAUL TEMPI
THE KELBY

Francis Henry Durbridge was born in Hull, Yorkshire, in 1912 and was educated at Bradford Grammar School. He was encouraged at an early age to write by his English teacher and went on to read English at Birmingham University. At the age of twenty-one he sold a play to the BBC and continued to write following his graduation whilst working as a stockbroker's clerk.

In 1938, he created the character Paul Temple, a crime novelist and detective. Many others followed and they were hugely successful until the last of the series was completed in 1968. In 1969, the Paul Temple series was adapted for television; and four of the adventures prior to this had been adapted for cinema, albeit with less success than radio and TV. Francis Durbridge also wrote for the stage and continued doing so up until 1991, when *Sweet Revenge* was completed. Additionally, he wrote over twenty other well-received novels, most of which were on the general subject of crime. The last, *Fatal Encounter*, was published after his death in 1998.

Also in this series

FRANCIS DURBRIDGE

Paul Temple and the Kelby Affair

COLLINS
CRIME
CLUB

COLLINS CRIME CLUB

An imprint of HarperCollins*Publishers*
1 London Bridge Street
London SE1 9GF
www.harpercollins.co.uk

This paperback edition 2015

First published in Great Britain by
Hodder & Stoughton 1970

A catalogue record for this book is
available from the British Library

ISBN 978-0-00-812568-4

Set in Sabon by Born Group using Atomik ePublisher from Easypress

Printed by CPI Group (UK) Ltd, Croydon CR0 4YY

MIX
Paper from
responsible sources
FSC® C007454

Chapter 1

SCOTT REED had intended to come at eleven o'clock: he arrived at ten. His Rover 2000 turned into the gravel drive as the clock above the stables was striking. The telephone call announcing his visit had sounded urgent, but then Scott Reed always left decisions until they became urgent. His office had telephoned at nine o'clock.

'Is that Mr Alfred Kelby?' the girl had asked.

'Yes,' said Alfred Kelby.

'I have a message from Mr Scott Reed. He is driving straight over to see you, and he expects to be there at eleven.'

Scott was one of the older school of publishers. He was slightly ashamed if a book sold well and he pretended that all their best sellers were the mistakes of his partner. Scott was a gentleman. He leaned over the back seat of his car and tenderly gathered up a packet. Then he came up to the house.

'Scott! Come in. I was just having breakfast.'

Kelby waved him into the library. One alcove in the book-littered room was clear and set for breakfast. Kelby removed a pile of manuscripts from an armchair and told Scott Reed to sit down. 'Coffee?' he asked.

1

'No thanks.' Scott sat on the edge of the seat. 'Or perhaps I will. Yes thanks.' He was unwrapping the packet as he changed his mind. 'I want you to read this, Kelby. It's a bombshell.'

It was a diary, bound in calf and written in green ink. The tiny, precisely rounded hand of a woman.

'Something you're going to publish?'

'Yes.' Scott Reed stared into his coffee. 'Well, we might. I was waiting for your opinion. And it depends on whether we can get an indemnity from all the living people who are mentioned in it. To make sure they don't sue us for libel.' He fidgeted slightly. 'What do you think?'

As an historian Kelby considered that very few diaries should be published. 'Serialisation in the Sunday papers,' he complained. 'It starts all the amateurs dabbling in history, writing letters. Clutters up scholarship.' His voice died away as he browsed through the yellowing pages. 'Good gracious me! Who was this woman? I take it the writer was a woman?'

'Yes. Lord Delamore's mistress.'

'Lord Delamore?' Kelby looked pleased. 'I knew him.' He read through a few more pages with intense fascination. But gradually he was frowning and clucking his tongue. 'This isn't history, it's downright scandal. Does she have much to say about the way he died? That was the great mystery of 1947.'

'She says a lot about that.' Scott Reed rose to leave. 'Perhaps you could read it through and have supper with me on Thursday?' He smiled distractedly. 'You can sign the release then.'

'Release?' Kelby was obviously delighted. 'Am I mentioned in this?'

'I'm afraid so.' Scott was edging his way to the door.

'I say, are you off already? I wanted you to meet my son, Ronnie. I don't think you've—'

2

'I'm sorry, Kelby, I haven't been to the office yet. I'm late. When does Ronnie go back to the States?'

'Well,' Kelby began hesitantly, 'he may be staying in England—'

'Good. Bring him with you on Thursday evening. My wife will be pleased to see him.' Scott Reed patted the diary. 'And don't lose that, for God's sake. We haven't been allowed to make a copy until the contract is signed.'

Kelby was protesting that copies were an historical imperative, but Scott Reed was scuttling across the lawn like a white rabbit, looking anxiously at his watch and eventually scrambling into the driving seat of the Rover. He hooted twice on the horn and vanished towards Melford Cross.

Alfred Kelby was a distinguished historian: he looked like a don and in fact he had been one until he found that it was interfering with his work. He was sixty-three and had too little time left for teaching thick-headed students. He now confined his lecturing to rare and highly paid television appearances, and spent most of his days researching a life of Neville Chamberlain. He ambled back to the alcove in the library, to finish his cold toast and marmalade.

It was early spring and low shafts of sunlight were penetrating the dusty corners of the library. Those intimations of summer that usually made him feel optimistic in March, that reconciled him to the rural remoteness of Melford House. But after the briefest glance at the larch trees opposite the window he was browsing again through Scott Reed's diary. He didn't hear Tracy Leonard come in.

'The post has arrived,' she announced. 'There's a reply from Ted Mortimer.'

It should have an index, of course. Kelby had instinctively turned to look up Chamberlain in the index. These amateurs, dabbling in history. Not that Chamberlain had any connection with the Delamore affair.

'I said there's a reply from Ted Mortimer.'

'Mortimer?' Kelby smiled, because she was attractive, especially for a secretary. 'What does he want?' Severe, but that was all part of her efficiency thing. Like her habit of slightly bullying him. Tracy Leonard was efficient.

'He wants to talk to you about the loan.'

'That means he still can't repay me.'

'Presumably. And I'm not surprised.'

Tracy Leonard sat at her desk and crossed her legs with elegant disdain. She flicked open her notebook and leaned forward to write. It made Kelby feel slightly sad that the curve of her thighs against the chair should be so perfect. They had worked together for many years, yet he still felt a pang when she came into the room, when he saw that sweeping gesture with her brown hair. He would never totally know the girl now, and the pangs made him feel like an elderly reprobate. Kelby wondered whether she had a lover, but he didn't dare ask. She had become inviolable.

'Shall I telephone and make an appointment for you to see him?'

Kelby nodded. She had admired him once, and Kelby had thought himself in love with the girl. He remembered her embraces that summer and found the memory painful. To her it obviously meant almost nothing, except that if she thought about it she would probably despise him. He was a foolish old man.

'Tell him I might drop in at Galloway Farm this afternoon. At about half past four.'

She had been a softly spoken and submissive girl until that afternoon when Ted Mortimer had burst into the library

4

while they were working. He had made a scene, shouted his accusations, and Tracy had never forgotten them. That was why Kelby hated the man when he thought about it. He rarely did think about it. He picked up the diary from the table.

'You look pale,' said Tracy. 'Wouldn't it be simpler to put the whole business into the hands of your solicitor?'

'No, that would be vindictive. He probably hasn't the money, and it wouldn't help anybody to sue him.'

There was nothing submissive about her face at the moment, her long mouth tight with disapproval. Perhaps she was vindictive, he decided, unless she wanted to save him pain.

'I don't have any other appointments, do I?' He smiled and made a conscious effort to become his old impish, happy self. He saw himself as mischievously cheerful. 'I can make this afternoon.'

'Yes, there's only the council meeting at half past eleven this morning, then you're free for the day.'

She was looking at the calf-bound diary, trying to see what had been so absorbing him. It was sheer perversity of Kelby to pick it up and put it secretively in his briefcase. 'I'll read this during the meeting,' he chuckled. 'More interesting than education business.'

'It looks like a diary,' she said casually.

'Just something Scott Reed wants me to look at. They're thinking of publishing it.'

Kelby left her feeling pleased with himself. His simple pleasure at thwarting her survived even seeing Ronnie come down the stairs, in his pyjamas, at half past ten.

'Aren't you dressed yet?' he asked automatically, but his mind was elsewhere. He would leave Tracy Leonard to squash the wastrel son.

'Don't worry, father, it's on the agenda.'

As Kelby left the house he could hear his son attempting his irresistible charm on the secretary. 'How romantic you make that sound, Miss Leonard. "There's nothing in the post for you, Mr Kelby." That sentence is the basis of our relationship.'

'We don't have a relationship, Mr Kelby.'

'You wait till I land a plum job, Miss Leonard, then you'll be impressed.'

'I certainly shall be.' Her voice was wholly discouraging. 'At the moment you don't even receive letters saying the position has been filled.'

Kelby was walking towards the garage, but then he glanced at the sky and decided to walk. He had meant to ask Scott Reed about a job for Ronnie; perhaps one of Scott's competitors needed a charming young man to hasten their flight into bankruptcy. But Kelby hated asking favours. He felt relieved that the subject was postponed until Thursday. Ronnie deserved a chance, but Kelby wondered whether the chance shouldn't have been given him ten years ago – when his mother had died. Kelby quickly pushed the past to the back of his mind.

There was plenty of time to walk to the village. Forty minutes. And anyway Kelby was only a co-opted member of the education subcommittee. He paused at the gate and spoke to Leo Ashwood. Leo was the gardener, handyman, butler, the whole team of male servants, who had been attached to Melford House ever since Kelby had bought the place. Ashwood and his wife had come with the house. Leo understood about nature.

'It's weather like this, Leo, that reconciles me to the rural remoteness of the country.'

'Yes, sir.'

Leo was the stolid type. Thickset, forty, and not plagued with the need to express himself.

'I like this time of year. Nobody ever declares a war in March.'

'No, sir.'

Kelby went off down the lane. He wasn't really a countryman. There were birds in the hedgerow, in the poplars, but Kelby couldn't be sure what they were, and he didn't like to ask. He hummed happily to himself. He was a man with no problems.

'Excuse me, am I right for Greatrex Lane?'

A man who looked like a doctor was calling from the car window. 'Yes,' said Kelby. 'It's about half a mile down the hill. On the right, just before you reach the village.'

'Melford Grammar School?'

'That's halfway down the lane. You can't miss it.'

An ambulance came speeding towards them, klaxon sounding, and it skidded to a halt on the wrong side of the road. 'Greatrex Lane?' the driver shouted.

'Follow me,' said the doctor.

Kelby decided to exert his authority. 'Has something happened at the school? I ought to know. I'm on the board of governors.'

'A fire,' the doctor said. 'It sounds like a bad one.' He drove grimly off down the hill.

'I say! Wait a minute!'

'Do you want to come with us?' asked the ambulance driver. 'I suppose it will be all right, you being on the board of governors.'

'Thanks.'

Kelby clambered into the back of the ambulance. A nurse and a male attendant hung on to him as they sped away. It was a bumpy ride. Kelby settled in the corner by the stretchers clutching his briefcase.

'Have you been called in from Oxford?' he asked conversationally.

Through the darkened windows he could see the telegraph poles and the occasional cottages whizzing by. It was a gloomy view. The school in the distance looked positively gothic, a sombre monument to the Victorian spirit of self-improvement. But Kelby couldn't see any fire. There were boys playing unconcernedly in the playing fields and as they flashed past the school a master was walking casually across the courtyard.

'That was the school,' said Kelby.

The male attendant sounded bored. 'Just relax, Mr Kelby, and nobody will hurt you.'

'Now look here—'

'Shut up, or somebody *will* hurt you.'

Kelby remained in the corner by the stretchers clutching his briefcase while the ambulance continued its journey.

Chapter 2

PAUL TEMPLE stepped off the VC 10 at Heathrow airport with a feeling of relief. He had liked America as usual, its pace and enthusiasm had been invigorating. But he welcomed London for its coolness and its casualness.

'Have you anything to declare, Mr Temple?' asked the customs officer.

Paul Temple nodded. 'It's nice to be back in England.'

He had been on a promotional tour, making personal appearances and giving interviews all the way down to California, to boost the sales of his latest novel. He had been on early morning chat shows in Pocatello, Idaho, had given radio interviews in Omaha, Nebraska, and had signed several thousand copies of the book along the east coast. But the interviewers never seemed to have read his books. They had only heard the gossip.

'Tell me, Mr Temple, why do you get involved in real investigations?'

'I try not to—'

'Don't the police in England resent your intrusion?'

Paul had laughed. 'Indeed they do.'

A women's writing circle in the middle west had demanded to know why English small town life was so much duller than Peyton Place. 'Do you think that murder is a dying art?' they had demanded.

After fifteen days Paul Temple had arrived back in New York and he still didn't know what a nickie hokie or a scoopie doo were. He had become tired of hearing that the English are so God-damned polite, and eventually he decided to take offence when a gossip columnist described him as an Englishman in the Empire-building tradition. Paul retorted that the gossip columnist was an American in the Empire State Building tradition. The man had simply laughed. The Americans are so God-damned good humoured.

Glancing at his reflection in the terminal lounge window, Paul decided that the Empire-building eyes were tired and the tall, lithe figure was slightly crumpled. Another week in America and he would have begun to look his age.

Steve and Scott Reed were waiting for him outside the Overseas Building. The publisher was looking like a worried terrier, as usual, but Paul Temple waved happily. The sight of his wife always made him feel quite euphoric.

'Darling,' she cried. 'Hello! How are you?'

'Steve!' He embraced her gratefully. 'I hadn't realised how I would miss you.' He shook hands with Scott Reed and sat in the back of the Rover. He knew that this wasn't simply a chauffeur service: Scott was in some kind of trouble. But that could wait. Paul Temple took his wife's hand and listened peacefully to the news about London. There really wasn't any news, which was its charm. Nothing had changed.

'How did the personal appearances go?' Steve asked, almost as an afterthought.

'Pretty quickly.'

She laughed. 'I knew as soon as I saw you that things had gone well.' She nodded wisely. 'You needed a holiday.'

'Holiday?'

He turned in mock disgust to Scott Reed.

'All right, Scott. You didn't come out to the airport to save my petrol. What's wrong?'

The Rover swerved momentarily. 'Wrong? Nothing.' The Mini behind them stopped hooting and Scott Reed settled into the slow lane. Motorways were for people with stronger nerves than his. 'I'm worried about Alfred Kelby.'

'The historian? I've met him . . .'

'Several times,' Steve intruded. 'Don't you remember that dinner party we went to with Scott just before Christmas? He has that marvellous housekeeper and she did a delicious coq au vin—'

'What about Kelby?'

'He's disappeared,' said Steve.

Paul Temple lived in a mews house. It was the kind of humble property that had suddenly become very fashionable a few years after the war, and was now extraordinarily expensive. When the garage had been a stable Paul's study had been the hayloft. The living room was the same room as the study but three steps up, above the kitchen and the entrance hall. The windows looked out across the Chelsea embankment and the Thames. It was mid-afternoon when they arrived from the airport. Paul led the way into the smartly modern house feeling a warm sense of homecoming.

'Sit down, Scott, and put your nervous system together,' he said.

Paul prided himself that in spite of the books and the paintings, the sharply contemporary furniture that Steve had installed, the mementoes and *objets d'art* of travel, the first floor was a workroom. A supremely comfortable workroom, but a workroom. The massive leather-topped desk set the tone of the place, he felt. That was where he worked.

He looked down at the silent typewriter and smiled. He had thought of a brilliant plot when he was in America. Tomorrow he would start work. This wouldn't simply be a murder story, but a study of murder.

'Steve,' he sighed, 'ask Kate to drum up some coffee. Poor old Scott is looking as if he needs it.'

Scott Reed sat in one of the egg-shaped Swedish chairs. 'Of course I'm worried about Kelby,' he said hollowly, his voice lost in the acoustic vacuum of the chair. 'But that's not all there is to it. He had a diary.'

'I beg your pardon?' Paul beckoned him to lean forward. His mime had improved since the chairs had been installed. 'I can't hear you.'

'Temple,' he shouted, 'if I asked you to name the three most important men in this country during the past fifty years, who would you name?'

'No need to shout.' He sat at his desk and decided upon Churchill, Bevan and Lloyd George. 'Now tell me who I am supposed to say.'

'Lord Delamore.'

Paul Temple laughed. 'Nonsense, Scott. If he hadn't been murdered so mysteriously in 1947 nobody would remember who he was. As a diplomat he was just another Old Etonian. It was the scandal of all those orgies in the shooting lodge that made him into a national figure.'

'Maybe. Anyway, about two months ago I met a woman called Bella Spender,' Scott Reed shouted. 'She lives in the South of France. I was staying there with some friends and—well, we became quite friendly.'

Paul was baffled. 'Bella Spender?'

'Yes. You won't have heard of her, Paul, but you should have heard of her sister, Margaret Spender.'

'Wasn't she Lord Delamore's secretary?'

'That's right.' Scott Reed leaned back in the chair and whispered sepulchrally: 'But she wasn't only his secretary. She was also his mistress.'

Steve came in with three cups of coffee and set them down on the glass-topped table. Her interest was immediately aroused by that part of the conversation she had heard.

'Margaret Spender kept a diary,' Scott Reed continued. 'A very detailed diary about her friendship with Lord Delamore and the lives of that whole set. It's absolutely scandalous. You've no idea what those bright middle-aged things got up to just after the war. I mean, that was when rationing was still with us—' He turned slightly pink as he realised that Steve was amused.

'Go on,' said Steve, 'it sounds fascinating.'

'Well, about two months ago I had a phone call from Bella Spender. She was over here, staying at Claridges, and she asked me to go round and see her. So I went, because we had been quite friendly, and she gave me the diary.'

'How had she come by the diary?' asked Paul.

'Her sister, Margaret Spender, had died. She was killed in an air crash a few months ago.'

'And why did she give you the diary?' Paul insisted.

Steve laughed. 'Because Scott is a publisher, darling.' She was enjoying the story. 'I'm surprised that Margaret herself hadn't tried to have it published. The mystery surrounding Lord Delamore's death is one of the most fascinating in the history of murder.'

Paul agreed. 'True-life mysteries sell very well. Did the diary give any answers?'

13

'Yes, but I don't know what credence we could give them. I was hoping that Kelby would tell me how true the allegations might be.'

'Kelby? You mean he saw this diary?'

'I took it down to him, the day he disappeared.'

'Oh my God!'

Scott Reed had sprung from the womb-like chair and was flapping about the room like a moth. 'I had to get him to sign an indemnity, because he was a guest at the shooting lodge when Delamore was killed, and he is mentioned in the diary. But I wanted his opinion about the facts.' He shrugged abjectly and looked across the Thames. 'I was worried about publishing it, Paul. The diary was sensational, but it was also vicious. They were a fast-living set, I know, but I couldn't believe they were quite so nasty. In the end I decided to ask Alfred Kelby whether the diary was accurate. On Monday morning I drove out to Melford Cross and gave him the diary to read.'

Paul Temple waited for a moment, but nothing more was said.

'Well?' asked Paul. 'What else?'

'Nothing. Kelby is missing, and so is the diary.'

Chapter 3

THE town hall in Melford Cross had been built in 1909, to celebrate the sudden promotion of its occupants from parish vestrymen to borough councillors. It was absurdly grand for the cluster of villages it served. As he went up the twenty-four steps to its entrance Paul Temple half expected the doors to open and two town criers to eject Larry the Lamb. Instead a retired sergeant major in grey uniform saluted and asked if he could help, governor.

'I'd like to see the town clerk. I'm Paul Temple.'

A painting of the first mayor in all his finery glared down the luxurious winding staircase. The cream and green colour scheme of the interior added a touch of Regency to the atmosphere. It seemed a shame that the building was so silent. The civic splendour of a bygone age. Paul followed the man down hushed corridors to an office looking on to the town square.

'Mr Temple? I'm Ballard, town clerk. How can I help you?'

They shook hands and Paul sat in a winged leather armchair. The town clerk looked genuinely pleased to see him, which increased Paul's suspicion that all the other rooms in the building were empty. Ballard was old, absent minded and extremely thin.

15

Perhaps when the place had been evacuated they had forgotten to advise him, they may have even thought he had retired.

'Things seem very quiet,' said Paul.

'It's all this local government reorganisation. Most of our work has been taken over, and the staff have gone with the work. That's centralisation, Mr Temple.'

'But you still administer education from here—'

'No,' Ballard interrupted. 'I suppose you've come about Mr Kelby. He's a co-opted member of the subcommittee for this region. A very good man, very entertaining.'

'Could you tell me what was on the agenda for Monday's meeting?'

'Nothing.'

'You don't think he would have been kidnapped to prevent him from attending the meeting? Or to put pressure on him to support some local issue?'

The town clerk was amused by the suggestion. 'Certainly not. At all our meetings Mr Kelby is in a minority of one.' His face was creased with happy appreciation. 'I don't think Mr Kelby is really in favour of education. He thinks it corrupts young minds, prevents them from learning and exploring.' He chuckled. 'Nobody takes Mr Kelby seriously in Melford Cross.'

Paul wondered why he was on the subcommittee.

'Prestige, I suppose, and the school children love him. He's very good at speech days.'

Paul asked about the publicity attending their subcommittee meetings.

'You mean, would anybody know that he had a meeting that morning? Yes, anybody could have known. The meetings of each council cycle are published in the local press. If anybody wanted to know we would tell them and keep no record of the fact. They aren't secret.'

'Thanks,' said Paul. He rose to leave. 'You've been very helpful.'

'I realised what you wanted to know.' He showed Paul to the door and shook hands. 'The police inspector asked the very same questions. He even asked why the building was so quiet. But he was rude, he cracked a joke about Larry the Lamb.'

Charlie Vosper was in charge of the case. He was at Melford House interviewing his suspects when Paul called on him fifteen minutes later. Charlie was a copper of the old school, not a bureaucrat. He was a good copper because he knew crooks, he respected them – the ones who were good at their job, and he even liked a lot of them. If Charlie hadn't joined Scotland Yard and become an inspector he could have been a successful underworld boss. Paul Temple knew him of old. They even liked each other.

'What do you want, Temple?' Vosper asked rudely.

'Just thought you might need some help.'

Charlie Vosper nodded. 'Like I need a week in hospital. Do you know this chap Kelby?'

'Slightly.'

'Come into the library and tell me about him.'

Paul approved of the carved oak and the obvious solidity of the place. It indicated an old-fashioned taste for the good things of life. 'Kelby seems quite a wealthy man,' he said as he sat in the chair by the window. He could see the chauffeur–handyman on the lawn: a thickset fellow who was obviously a hard worker.

'Did you think he was poor?'

'No. But I thought he might be more superficial than these surroundings suggest.' When Scott Reed had gone Paul had spent the evening reading history. It was one way of getting to grips with the missing man. And he had found that Kelby's

17

books were like his television appearances, so brilliant that you suspected him of showing off. He was provocative and witty. Not quite the academic historian.

'He's a shabby-looking bloke, I gather,' said the inspector. 'Lives a pretty dull life here in Melford.'

'Yes. I was referring to his mind.'

'Oh.'

Paul Temple talked for several minutes about the Kelby he had met and how their lives had occasionally intersected. But it didn't add up to much. On the occasions when Kelby had been accompanied by a woman she had been thirty years younger than himself, which had also seemed ostentatious.

'Young people have livelier minds,' said Charlie Vosper. 'Why should he be compelled to go about with women of his own age? He's a widower.'

'Really? I didn't know he had been married.'

'His wife died ten years ago. He has a son, Ronnie, who is staying here at the moment. He's on holiday from America.'

'Oh yes, of course. Scott Reed said something about avoiding the son; Kelby was fishing after a job for him.'

'Mr Kelby and his son didn't like each other,' Vosper said grimly.

When Paul Temple saw the young man he could understand why. Ronnie was fair haired and charming in an obvious, straightforward way, and his mind was totally conventional. He must have been a grave disappointment to Kelby.

'Do you think my father has been murdered?' Ronnie asked.

Inspector Vosper was at his most intimidating. 'Why, do you think he might have been?'

'I don't know. If he'd just been kidnapped we should have heard now, shouldn't we? It's five days since he left to attend that council meeting.' He lit a cigarette and glanced nervously at the constable who was writing everything down. 'The kidnappers would have asked us for the ransom, or something.'

'The other alternative is that he simply cleared off. People are doing that all the time, they simply leave home. It isn't against the law.'

Ronnie shrugged. 'So what are you doing here?'

'Making bloody sure, son. What did you do with yourself on Monday?'

'Monday? Oh, I got up, drifted about—'

'What time did you get up?'

'Half past nine.'

'And where did you drift?'

'Around the house until lunchtime. I usually spend the morning trying to seduce Miss Leonard. She's my father's assistant. Then when I fail I go down to the pub for lunch or over to the golf club. It consoles me, you understand, restores my faith in my virility. On Monday I went over to the golf club and went round with the pro. There was nobody else about and I don't have any friends in Melford. I came back to the house feeling sorry for myself.'

'Time?'

'Oh, between four and five. Then I wrote off for a job.'

'What job?'

'With the Arts Council of Great Britain.'

Paul found that his attention was straying as the routine interviews proceeded. He ought to have been interested, as Vosper said, to watch somebody else at work. But Paul hadn't yet acclimatised himself to the English times. In America they were hours behind and they never went to bed.

He stopped yawning when Tracy Leonard came into the room. She was tall and twenty-five and had straight brown

19

hair. She wasn't the type to take bullying from Charlie Vosper. She didn't take to the bluff, fatherly manner either.

'Mr Kelby is a historian, inspector. He needs his books and his papers, otherwise he can't work. And he had promised Neville Chamberlain to his publisher by October.'

'Neville Chamberlain?' said Vosper blankly.

'He was prime minister before the war.'

'I know who he was, Miss Leonard! I just fail to see what Neville Chamberlain has to do with your employer's disappearance!'

She smiled patiently, a demure advertisement for the very best toothpaste. 'I am explaining to you that Mr Kelby cannot have left home voluntarily. He is writing a book on Neville Chamberlain, and obviously he will have done absolutely no work this week. He has to work here, among all this.' She gestured eloquently at the muddle of the library.

Charlie Vosper took three deep breaths and composed his leathery face back into a friendly expression. 'Well, that seems to imply that he was removed by force. After all, if he were lost or had fallen ill the local police would have found him. They're known from here to London as the Blue Berets.' He chuckled to prove his good nature, the policeman with a sense of humour.

'How did you spend last Monday?' he asked her.

'I worked all day. I have a room in what Mr Kelby calls the east wing. It's a room built on to the side of the house. I came through at nine o'clock and opened the post, sorted out the day's work . . .' She had worked for Kelby for several years and her routine was established.

'When did you realise Mr Kelby was missing?'

Tracy Leonard smiled. She regarded that as a silly question. 'He was due back from the town hall around one, and he didn't return. If you mean when did I really become worried, that was in the evening. Ronnie Kelby and I spent half the evening doing a tour of Melford. We searched everywhere he was likely to be. And then at about ten o'clock we went to the police.'

'Did Ronnie Kelby,' the inspector asked surprisingly, 'share your concern?'

'I think so. He went for three hours without making a pass at me.'

'How galling for you.'

'It's like having fleas, you don't notice them after a while.'

Tracy Leonard had been one of Kelby's brightest students; she had stayed on to do research with him when all her contemporaries had taken jobs as schoolteachers, and she had given up university life when Kelby had. She thought he was a great historian.

'Have you any idea why he would have been taken by force?'

'I assume somebody wanted to get their hands on that diary.'

'What diary?'

'The diary that Scott Reed left with him on Monday morning. It seemed to be an important historical document.'

Charlie Vosper rose slowly to his feet. 'You didn't tell me anything about a diary.'

'You didn't ask me. It was apparently rather valuable.'

Paul intervened tactfully to save the girl from the massive wrath of the law. 'Rather scandalous, actually. I should think a lot of people would give a lot to have it suppressed.'

'You knew about this?' Charlie shouted.

'I assumed everybody knew.'

Charlie Vosper was turning a terrible shade of mauve.

*

'No, he wasn't shouting, Mrs Ashwood. The inspector has one of those voices that carries a long way.' Paul Temple lifted the ladle to his lips and tasted the stew. 'Especially when he's angry. This is a stew like they used to make it in the depths of the country, Mrs A.'

'Mr Kelby is very partial to it, sir.'

'I'm not surprised.' Paul continued his approving tour of the kitchen. 'How long have you been with Mr Kelby?'

'Oh, it must be more than ten years now. Leo and I moved in when Mrs Kelby was taken ill. That was a sad time for Mr Kelby and he found he needed help. He's such a good man. We did everything we could to keep this a home for him, especially after she died. Do you think he'll be all right?'

'I trust so, Mrs Ashwood. I really hope so.' She was a large, motherly woman and she was clearly devoted to her employer. Paul sensed the grief that such disruptions of normal domesticity can cause; suddenly Kelby was a human being and it mattered that he should be well.

'Is Leo your husband?'

'Yes, that's right.'

'I saw him working in the grounds.'

'He's a hard worker. It takes his mind off the trouble. Leo is more like a friend of Mr Kelby than just the handyman.' She allowed a brief laugh to ripple through her ample body. 'Mr Kelby always says that Leo taught him to be a countryman. They're very close.'

It was relaxing in the kitchen. Gladys Ashwood lived in a nice world of nice people. She was sympathetic about Mr Ronnie. 'Well, he was devoted to his mother. Her death was such a blow that he needed somebody to blame. He blamed Mr Kelby. But they've made it up now. Mr Kelby was so pleased that his son came home the other week. There's even talk of Mr Ronnie staying . . .' She liked Tracy Leonard: 'Such a brilliant girl and ever so much the lady. She's been here for nearly five years . . .' None of these nice people would ever harm Mr Kelby. The only person she had bad words to say about was Ted Mortimer.

'I feel responsible in a way,' she was saying. 'Ted Mortimer used to be very close with my husband and me. We used to see a lot of him. But he's not a countryman. He was in the merchant navy.'

Paul was drinking a cup of tea she had poured him and he scarcely heard her story about the row Kelby had with the neighbouring farmer. 'Mr Kelby was going over there on Monday afternoon,' she said, and the words registered with a sudden shock.

'What did you say, Mrs Ashwood?'

'To see Ted Mortimer. He was going over to Galloway Farm—'

'Did he ever arrive?'

'I couldn't say.'

'What was their row about?'

'I wouldn't know, Mr Temple, but they do say in the village that there was a quarrel about money. We don't see Ted Mortimer any more, you see, and I'm not one to gossip myself—'

'Of course you aren't, Mrs Ashwood. But you're a wonderful raconteur. Excuse me if I dash away.' He squeezed her shoulder affectionately. 'By the way, this is my card. If you do remember any gossip, please let me know. I'm a devil of a gossip myself.'

She was laughing complacently as he left the kitchen and collided in the hall with Charlie Vosper. The inspector had come running from the library.

'Where are you off to?' Vosper asked suspiciously.

'Me? Oh, I thought I'd make a tour of the neighbouring farms. It hasn't been done, has it?'

'No, it hasn't. Would you mind driving with me, Temple? I'd like to be sure I know all that you know before we search Ted Mortimer's place. I like to keep abreast.'

They walked across the drive towards the police car with studied casualness. But the inspector reached it first.

Chapter 4

'OF course there never was such a diary, my dear. How could there be when Dickie never had such a mistress? Dickie had his faults, I'd be the first to admit them: he was a bore and he danced abominably, but I never noticed people rushing off to enter up their diaries whenever Dickie trod on their corns. What did you say this person's name was?'

Steve persevered with the assignment. 'Miss Spender. Margaret Spender.'

'Never heard of her!'

'She was your husband's secretary.'

The frail old lady said: 'Oh!' like an ancient bird sighting a small field mouse. '*That* Miss Spender. I always felt sorry for her. She was a big girl. We called her the last of the big Spenders.' Her eyes sparkled with malicious life.

'Miss Spender did keep a diary for those ten years,' said Steve, 'and of course that included the period after the war when your husband was murdered.'

'Killed, dear. It could have been an accident. I expect it gave her something to do in the evenings.'

'And now that she is dead her sister has decided to publish it.'

'How very demeaning.'

Steve had felt slightly nervous when she arrived at Delamore House. But she had made an appointment with Lady Delamore's secretary, which Paul had said was significant. She's worried, he had said, or else she wants to know what is going on. A butler had shown Steve into the drawing room; and then Lady Delamore had bustled in calling for Simpson to bring tea.

'We'll have tea early today,' she had said pedantically. It was only ten minutes to four. 'Mrs Temple looks as if she needs sustenance.'

She was not putting Steve at her ease.

'You young people are so thin these days. I'm thin, but then I'm eighty-five. When I was your age I had a generous bosom and a bottom you could really sit on.'

'You must have led a busy life in those—'

'It must be all this unisex that you people go in for these days. It makes everybody thin.'

The butler brought in tea at that point. It gave Steve an excuse to change the subject. She talked about the diary although Lady Delamore's attention soon wandered.

'How do you come to be involved in this?' she suddenly demanded.

'My husband is a crime writer, and it was his publisher who acquired the diary.'

'Crime, eh?' She laughed derisively. 'It's a little late for solving any of the mysteries which surrounded my husband's death. Those of us who are still alive have forgotten what little we knew.'

'Nobody is trying to solve anything, Lady Delamore,' Steve said provocatively. 'The solutions are all given in the diary.'

'Which has disappeared, you said?'

'A man has disappeared, Lady Delamore. The historian, Alfred Kelby. The diary is incidental, although if we found that we might also find Mr Kelby. My husband wondered whether you, or some of your friends, might be being blackmailed. Whoever has this diary might try to extort money by it.'

'I never pay blackmailers,' she pronounced aphoristically, 'and none of my friends have any money. I'm sorry I couldn't be more help.'

Steve helped herself to another tea cake. 'Alfred Kelby was reading the diary to give his opinion on its historical authenticity,' she said.

'I don't understand. Do you mean he could confirm that my husband was really murdered? And murdered by whomever Miss Spender accuses? Surely if Mr Kelby knew that he should have said in 1947, when poor Sir Philip Tranmere was arrested. I believe there was a Mr Kelby in the party up at the shooting lodge at the time, but I don't remember that he was really in with the best people.'

Steve suggested that Mr Kelby could find the diary explanation convincing or not. 'He would know the people involved, and he might be a better witness than you, Lady Delamore, on the subject of Miss Spender.'

'What would a historian know of my poor late husband's sexual relationships? This publisher should have asked me. I could have told him that Dickie's morals were above reproach. He snored in his sleep and his feet smelled. Those are not characteristics that attract stray women. What is more, after three whiskies he fell fast asleep. What would he want with a mistress? I never knew a man who slept as much as Dickie.'

Lady Delamore had already spent eighty-five years of her life keeping people in their place. Steve found it almost impossible to guess whether she was worried, guilty, or sublimely above the contemporary world. But just as she was about to leave the butler appeared.

'Excuse me, my lady. Sir Philip Tranmere is on the telephone.'

'I'll ring him back, Simpson.'

'He says that it is most urgent, my lady.'

Lady Delamore sighed. 'The silly man. It is not urgent to me. Tell him that everything is perfectly in order, and I'll ring him this evening. Mrs Temple is about to leave.'

Steve left. After the afternoon's ordeal it was almost a shock to see the mini and maxi skirts and fashionable long hair, people on the streets who belonged unmistakably to the 1970s.

Paul was still out when she reached home. So Steve helped Kate with the housework and allowed her mind to freewheel over the things Lady Delamore had said. She had a record sleeve to design by Monday, but she didn't want to become absorbed in anything else until she had talked to Paul. He arrived shortly after nine o'clock to find Steve doodling at the drawing board.

'Lady Delamore didn't feel worried or guilty, I'm sure of that,' Steve assured him. 'In fact I don't think she gives a damn about anything or anybody. I only hope I'll be like that when I'm eighty-five. She was so dreadful she was rather splendid.'

Paul laughed. 'I'm sure that when you're eighty-five you'll be absolutely appalling!'

'Flatterer.'

'It's nice to be back.' He poured himself a whisky and sat beside Steve. 'Hello, have you been commissioned to do some work?'

'Yes, I saw Jeremy while you were away.' She smiled quickly. 'He said the work was flowing in again. Design looks up. Britain will look a better place to live in—'

'That sounds like Jeremy. While I was pounding along the Atlantic seaboard earning dollars for Britain Jeremy was seducing my wife with record sleeves.'

Steve laughed. 'I sat here night after night, thinking of you and knitting in front of the fire. I read *Dylan Thomas in America* to keep myself company. But did you miss me?'

'I'll say I did, my darling.' He kissed her cheek. 'Next time I see Jeremy I'll punch him on the nose. Do you want some whisky?'

'Not at the moment. I've spent a hideous afternoon to discover what that old crone knew about the diary. So listen and sound interested.'

'Mm. Tell me.'

'I think the diary is probably in her possession.'

Paul stood up in amazement. 'Really? Steve, you're marvellous! How did you establish that?'

She shrugged. 'I didn't. Call it feminine intuition.'

'Oh, that. You mean you're guessing.'

'I'm convinced of it. Can I have some brandy?'

Paul went across to the sideboard and opened a bottle of brandy. 'I suppose she would be the number one suspect for stealing it. But I can't see an eighty-five-year-old woman kidnapping Kelby.' He looked at the bottle for a moment, then said quietly: 'Did I tell you? We found Kelby this afternoon.'

Charlie Vosper had driven like a stunt man in a silent film to reach Ted Mortimer's farm. He had telephoned for two constables to conduct a search of the premises. The constables arrived from the opposite direction at the same time as Charlie Vosper swung into Galloway Farm and narrowly missed three hens out for a walk. They drove in convoy past the barn and cattle sheds alongside a field of sheep to the rambling farmhouse. By the time the two cars had skidded to a halt Ted Mortimer was already in the doorway.

'Do you realise it's dangerous to drive at that speed?' he demanded.

He was a big man with a red, weather-beaten face. His arms were tattooed with swords and snakes. An aggressive man who was none too pleased to see the police.

'What's all the panic?' he asked.

Charlie Vosper showed his identification. 'We're investigating the disappearance of Mr Alfred Kelby. I believe you knew him. He's been missing since Monday morning, and I wondered whether you could help us to locate him.'

Mortimer shook his head. 'I'm sorry, I can't. Kelby and I weren't really on visiting terms.'

'He was coming over here on Monday afternoon.'

'That's right. But he never arrived.'

Charlie Vosper stared at the farmer, deciding whether he was 'straight' or not. It was a careful examination and Paul could see why the man should glare so aggressively back.

'Do you mind if we look over your farm?'

Mortimer was ungracious. 'Go ahead if you must, but don't disturb my livestock. They aren't used to policemen.'

The farm was obviously run down. Ted Mortimer himself bore a grudge against the world, and his men bore a grudge against Ted Mortimer. The animals obviously didn't give a damn for anyone. It was something to do with the weather, Paul decided as he wandered round in the wake of the police. The weather was always bad for farmers.

'Bad weather for the crops,' he said conversationally to Ted Mortimer as they came out of the tractor shed.

'We're mainly livestock here,' he said. 'Dairy farm.'

Paul nodded. 'Shocking weather.'

The two constables had been through the rooms and attic and cellars of the house, without success. Of course a body could have been buried in the fields. But they went through the outhouses and ramshackle cattle sheds systematically. They found Kelby when they reached the barn.

The barn was built on two levels. The ground level was scattered with sacks of fertiliser and a set of disc harrows. On the upper level a rusty old bath kept company with an abandoned sewing machine, a child's rocking horse and an odd assortment of junk. One of the constables on the top level was leaning out of the loading bay as Charlie Vosper and Paul Temple reached the doors.

'He's down there,' the man called. 'The rain butt by the corner.'

Paul and the inspector ran to the back of the barn. The rain butt was very large, and unless you were deliberately searching you wouldn't have seen the hand resting over the edge by the drainpipe.

A police ambulance and a doctor were sent for, as well as the photographer and a fingerprint man from the lab. Paul Temple watched in fascination as the whole organisation moved smoothly into action. A constable stayed on duty by the body and the other took statements from the farm hands. It was such a routine operation for them that a man's violent death became almost an irrelevance.

'Nobody's been near this bloody barn for ten days. You can see it's hardly used at this time of year.'

Paul Temple realised that the farmer was still standing next to him. As the only other man without a part to play he had stayed helplessly by Paul's side, watching and feeling sorry for himself.

'When did you last see Mr Kelby alive?' Paul asked him.

'I saw him in the village about a week ago. But I didn't speak to him.'

'Why not?'

31

'I saw him first.'

'What does that mean?'

'What do you think it means? It means I avoided him.' Ted Mortimer stepped aside to allow the doctor to pass. They were about to move the body. It was a bloated, blue-hued impersonal thing, nothing more to do with Alfred Kelby. 'Wouldn't you avoid someone if you owed him two thousand quid, and you were up to your bloody ears in debt?'

Paul smiled thoughtfully. 'That's a good question. I think I probably would, Mr Mortimer.'

The farmer looked at him for a moment, not quite sure what to make of Paul's attitude. Then he turned away to stare at the ambulance. The stray hand was visible again, hanging below the white sheet.

'Did you know that Mr Kelby was coming to see you on Monday afternoon?'

'That stuck-up secretary of his telephoned; it was like announcing a royal visit. But Kelby didn't turn up.'

'Were you at home Monday afternoon and evening?'

'Yes,' Mortimer said angrily. 'And I didn't see anybody putting him in the rain butt. I would have sent them both packing if I had!'

'What time do your men go home?'

'At this time of the year about six o'clock. Now do you mind if I get some work done? I've a livelihood to earn.'

Ted Mortimer strode away to the house. Paul smiled to himself and went across to join Charlie Vosper. The ambulance was just departing, and Charlie was watching it go as he lit his pipe.

'Well?' asked Paul.

The inspector growled and carried on lighting his pipe. 'He's been in that water some time. Probably since Monday.'

'Was he drowned?' Paul asked.

'I don't know. We'll have to wait for the autopsy.' He threw a match into the ground level of the barn and watched to see whether it carried on burning. 'From the look of him I'd say that his neck was broken, but there's bound to have been a struggle. I'd like to know which happened first.'

Paul nodded. 'It would make quite a difference.'

'If he died of a broken neck he could have been killed elsewhere and then brought here later. That would be easier.'

'You're speculating, inspector.'

Charlie Vosper glared, caught out in an unpolicemanly act. 'Let's find a cup of tea, shall we?' he muttered.

Vosper led the way into Ted Mortimer's large flagstoned kitchen. Mortimer was sitting at the scrubbed wooden table staring at the bottle of beer before him. The kitchen, like the rest of the house, looked in need of a woman's hand. Paul guessed that the man's wife had left him years ago; he was not a warm and charming man.

'I'm afraid there's a little more to it than that, Mr Mortimer,' said the inspector. 'A dead man has been found on your farm. Can you tell me anything about it?'

'No, of course I can't.'

'Why did the dead man lend you money?'

Mortimer strode across to the refrigerator, his large farm boots clattering on the stone floor. 'Do you want some beer?' he asked. 'I'm afraid there isn't anything else . . .' They said no thanks. 'Alfred Kelby lent me two thousand pounds because I was broke. This farm is mortgaged to the last pig's tail. He wanted to help me.'

'Why?' Paul asked.

'How should I know? I suppose he wanted me to like him. Why do people usually lend money?'

Vosper sighed and looked at Paul. 'Perhaps we ought to be going. Mr Mortimer may remember something more helpful when the importance of this death has sunk into him. Coming back to the Kelby residence, Temple?'

Paul Temple shook his head. 'I want to get back to London. There are one or two things . . .' Then he remembered that the inspector had driven him over and that his car was still at Melford House. 'Oh well, perhaps I will. Let's ask Gladys Ashwood to make that cup of tea. She's a first-class cook.'

Charlie Vosper agreed. 'We'll have to break the news there. The son will have to make formal identification.'

Perhaps it was because breaking such news to anyone, a son or a secretary or even the handyman, is an unpredictable ordeal that they drove back slowly. Paul watched the passing countryside with a new sense of its strangeness. Darkness was already falling. He found himself wondering whether Kelby had died in pain.

'By the way, Charlie, we didn't find Kelby's briefcase, did we?'

'No, we didn't.'

They remained in the car when it drew up at Melford House. 'I suppose you were wondering about the diary.'

'As a matter of fact——'

'I think it's all a bit fanciful. I'm a simple copper, I believe in simple murders for simple motives. I don't see that Alfred Kelby would be murdered for a diary the same day as it was given to him. It's too much of a coincidence that he should have it in his briefcase, and from what I hear the publisher was the only man who knew he had it.'

'Yes, Charlie——'

'But I know you, Temple. You'll go sniffing after that diary, because you're a literary sort of gentleman. So get this straight. If you stumble across anything interesting I want to know. I don't care why you think it wouldn't interest me, and I don't mind you interrupting my routine work. You get straight on to me. Right?'

'Unambiguous, Charlie.'

Charlie climbed from the car muttering about literary bloody gentlemen and the gritty realism of police work.

The lights were on in the house. And while they had been talking a couple of white faces had appeared silhouetted in the windows. Paul felt distinctly inadequate as he saw Gladys Ashwood running across the forecourt towards the car. He knew she was going to be upset, and something of his feeling must have shown because she stopped a few yards away and just stared.

'He's dead?' she asked eventually.

Paul Temple put a hand on her shoulder. 'Let's go back inside, Mrs Ashwood.'

Her husband Leo was standing in the side doorway. 'What happened?' he asked hoarsely.

'I'm afraid Mr Kelby has been murdered.'

Leo muttered: 'Oh my God.' It was a pretty conventional reaction, but it was genuine, like his wife's tears. She sobbed in total incomprehension. After Paul and Leo had got her to the kitchen she asked the usual unanswerable questions, about who could do such a thing and why it was necessary.

'Where did you find him?' Leo demanded.

'In a barn on Ted Mortimer's farm.'

'Mr Kelby lent him two thousand pounds,' Leo said harshly. 'That's why he killed him. Did the police arrest the bastard?'

'Well no, they don't yet know who actually killed Mr Kelby.'

'They don't know?' he shouted angrily.

And in counterpoint his wife was whispering that Mr Kelby was such a wonderful person, always so thoughtful and kind to everyone. She couldn't believe it.

'Does Mr Ronnie know what's happened, sir?' asked Leo.

'Er yes, I think the inspector is telling him now. My goodness, Inspector Vosper will be wondering where I've got to. I told him I was off back to London. Well, look after your wife, Mr Ashwood. It's a tragic blow . . .'

'I just can't believe it,' she was sobbing. 'Poor Mr Kelby. And I was going to pick up his suit from the cleaners this afternoon. There are so many jobs to do, and there isn't any point now.'

'Go and pick up the suit,' Leo ordered gruffly. 'We're still working.'

As Paul slipped out of the house he found Scott Reed arriving in the black Rover. Paul greeted him with some surprise.

'I came to see whether they've found Kelby. I feel so responsible, having given him the diary to read. And I promised Bella Spender a decision today.' He was flapping. He wanted to say all the things on his mind in one speech. 'Has anything happened?'

'We found Kelby, but I'm afraid he's dead.'

Scott was silent and the colour drained from his face.

'We found him a couple of miles away, in a rain butt.'

'My God! I'd better go in and offer my condolences. I asked him to read that diary, you see.'

Paul watched him cross the drive and go uncertainly into the house. He looked a worried man. But he couldn't have foreseen that this would happen, Paul thought to himself as he drove away. It surely wasn't Scott's fault.

*

'Do you think I look like a unisex person?'

'Certainly not.' Paul was suddenly suspicious. 'Why? What would that make me?'

'I don't know. It was that awful dowager. She was being nasty about my trouser suit. She said I was thin.'

'So you are. It's all that slimming.'

'Paul! I thought you liked me to be beautiful?'

He laughed. 'You are beautiful. That's what I call a compact figure. It doesn't flop about all over the place. Let's go to bed. I haven't yet adjusted to English times.'

'I don't know what that means, but it sounds as if you shouldn't have had that extra brandy after the wine. Paul! Put me down!'

Kate Balfour bustled in from the kitchen, stopped abruptly and then bustled back. She removed her apron and crept silently from the house.

Chapter 5

PAUL TEMPLE was making notes for the book he had thought of in America. He was trying to decide whether *Crime and Punishment* was a thriller, and whether death was tragic. He wanted his murder to be a gratuitous act, rather than an *acte gratuité*, with about as much dramatic meaning as a car crash: that would be its significance. But perhaps he was becoming pompous. He went through into the kitchen and made a jug of coffee.

'Can you see any reason why Kelby's death should be connected with the diary?' he asked Steve. 'Or why he should have been killed because of a quarrel with Ted Mortimer? Maybe his son coming back from America at this precise moment has nothing to do with anything.'

Steve nodded patiently. 'What's the matter?'

'I just thought . . . well, he might have been killed by a tramp or a drink-crazed bank manager. Think of the great national pool of hatred that must exist against television performers; Kelby often lectured on television, and now perhaps he has paid the price of fame. The drunken bank manager then realised what he had done, panicked, and hid the body in the barn. Why should it all tie in with everything?'

'I know this mood of yours, Paul. You talk like this when you want to write the *Bleak House* of the twentieth century. The great Elizabethan novel. Sit down and let me pour the coffee. You'll soon feel better.'

Better! Words flooded into his mind and became jammed. Better?

'Kelby might have caught the handyman stealing the spoons. Ashwood. He might have been calling the police to arrest Ashwood.'

Steve was busy with the coffee. 'Yes, dear, he sounds a dubious character. I'd look into Mr Ashwood.' She nodded in vague encouragement.

'Darling, don't be silly. Ashwood wouldn't have killed him.'

'No, dear.' She rattled a few cups. 'That was your idea.'

'I simply wondered whether we were being too logical.'

'I know you did.'

Paul sat in his chair at the massive desk and stared at his notes. They were pompous. He went over and sat in the Swedish egg chair. *The Times* crossword puzzle. That would clarify the mind. He sipped his coffee and picked up the newspaper. He had nearly finished the crossword yesterday, which showed that his mind was confused. The egg chair shut out the world. He browsed contentedly through the paper.

'Historian dead in rain butt,' ran the headline. Paul read the story automatically:

'Alfred Kelby, the historian, was found upside down in a butt of water yesterday after a three day search by the police had led them to a farm two miles from Alfred Kelby's home in Melford Cross. The police are treating it as a case of murder . . .'

As the crossword was on the back page it meant you had to browse through the whole paper to reach it. Several pages later Paul glanced at the obituaries:

'Alfred Kelby was an idiosyncratic historian whose wayward and controversial career sometimes obscured the real scholarship which lay behind his work . . .'

There was no mention of Kelby's girlfriend. The young, extrovert blonde Paul had seen with him on those social occasions. Paul wondered why he hadn't come across her, or heard mention of her in Melford Cross.

'Steve!' he called. 'What happened to Kelby's girlfriend?'

She was only the other side of the room, but she scarcely heard his muffled voice.

'Darling!' He sprang into the room. 'Do you realise there's no woman in this case? That isn't natural.'

Steve smiled sweetly. 'What about me?'

'You don't count.'

'There's Tracy Leonard. I thought you were rather taken with her. Couldn't she have been involved?'

Paul grunted something about motives. 'I doubt if there was a romantic link between her and Kelby – someone else would have known if there were. Leo or Ronnie would have known. There wouldn't be much of a financial motive; I expect Ronnie stands to inherit what money there is. She's an independent girl. A promising young history student in her own right. If she were in trouble or bored with her work she would presumably marry and live happily ever after in Hendon.'

'So perhaps it was Ronnie, to lay his hands on the inheritance.'

'That wouldn't be a fortune,' said Paul. But he knew people had been murdered for less. He picked up the telephone and dialled Scott Reed's office. 'I'd rather find a woman in the case.'

He invited Scott to dinner.

'He'll know about the girl,' Paul explained to Steve. 'It was at one of his parties we met Kelby with that blonde girl on his arm. He'll know who she was, or who replaced her. Anyway I'd like to see Scott again. This case revolves around his missing diary. Kelby may have been killed by someone who was anxious to obtain that diary.'

'That's true,' said Steve. 'I wonder where it will end.'

Paul laughed. 'I don't think Scott Reed is in danger. They presumably have the diary now. Either Lady Delamore or a person unknown.'

But Steve was fascinated by the idea of a series of deaths arising out of the diary. It was an idea Paul had once used, the serial murder, in an early novel. For the rest of the day while she was alone in the house she convinced herself that it was Scott Reed's last night on earth.

Charlie Vosper's field headquarters were in Melford Cross opposite the town hall. It was a disused drill hall from the days when the county regiment was in full pride. Charlie had ten men, including two sergeants, with two cars and two telephones. From time to time the local inspector drifted resentfully in to check on progress, found they were getting nowhere and drifted happily out.

Paul passed him in the entrance and said: 'Good morning, Inspector Hobden. Delivering the morning report?'

'Huh.' He stopped in country fashion for a chat. 'Do you know what they've been doing? House-to-house statements.' He glanced up at the sky; it was cloudy but the breeze would soon clear things. It would be a bright afternoon. 'House-to-house questioning! That's all London boys can do. They don't know the area, so all they can do is fall back on routine. Huh.'

'Whereas,' Paul said, lingering, 'you've known all the people involved since they were so high.'

'Exactly.' He jammed the flat cap onto his head and stepped into the gravel forecourt. 'I've known them for years.'

'And what would you do, Inspector Hobden, if it were still your case?'

Hobden glanced right and left, and right again. 'I'd check on Ronnie Kelby, Mr Temple. Things have changed since he arrived. He's a comparative stranger, and between you and me, Mr Temple, he's a smooth one.'

Paul chuckled to himself as the man strode off towards the police station. He liked the way Hobden worked: it was uncomplicated and direct. He had said the same thing to Charlie Vosper about Paul – a stranger and a smooth one. He probably objected to Vosper for being a stranger, although nobody had ever called Charlie smooth.

Charlie was sitting on a table sticking pins in a map of the district and biting into a bacon sandwich.

'What do you want?'

'I thought you might be lonely out here among the natives.'

It was an impressive flurry of activity. The murderer, if he or she could see the concentrated effort, would have confessed on the spot.

'What's this about Ronnie Kelby?' he asked Charlie Vosper.

'Have you been talking to Hobden? He's a village bobby at heart; he doesn't understand crime. Do you know what he said about Ted Mortimer this morning? That Mortimer is a bit impetuous. What the hell, does he want to send Mortimer to bed without his supper?'

'So what about Ronnie Kelby?'

'He's a troublemaker. Apparently his father has changed, or rather had changed, since Ronnie came home from America. Inspector Hobden thinks it was Ronnie's fault that his father quarrelled with Mortimer.'

Paul nodded. 'But would Ronnie murder his dad?'

'That depends on how bad their relationship was ten years ago. He seems a bit impetuous and spoiled, to put it mildly.'

'Have you checked on him with the FBI?'

Charlie Vosper nodded. 'Nothing criminal, but he had come to their attention. He got into a fight in New York, and once in Boston he was arrested for being drunk and disorderly. Those are still crimes in America, but Ronnie boy got off. He's unstable.'

'Yes,' said Paul. 'Dangerous.'

A uniformed constable came hurrying over to the desk. 'Your helicopter has arrived, sir,' he announced disbelievingly. 'Apparently it's in a field behind the part-time library.'

'Right,' said Vosper. 'Let's go.'

The helicopter was surrounded by villagers who were all talking about moon landings. They were staring at the leather-clad pilot and chattering as if he wouldn't understand what they were saying about him. It was the most exciting event since a German plane had crashed on Armitage's farm in 1942, and none of them had actually seen that.

'Excuse me,' called Vosper. 'Make way, please.'

'What are we doing?' asked Paul.

'We? I'm spending an hour going across the fields around Ted Mortimer's farm. Are you coming?'

'What about insurance?'

Charlie Vosper gave him a withering glare and then climbed into the cockpit without answering. Paul followed him. It was a tiny RAF helicopter that sat two men and the pilot. Vosper and PC Anderson were the two men, so Paul huddled nervously on the floor. As the craft shuddered into the air and the crowd moved back in religious awe Paul succumbed to paranoia. He knew the inspector usually regarded him as a nuisance. It was a plot to kill him. The helicopter suddenly soared to two hundred feet in a vertical take-off and then shot forward towards Melford House.

'What are you grinning about?' Paul demanded.

'If I didn't know you as well as I do I'd think you were nervous.'

'I'm uncomfortable, wedged here in the corner. What happens if the door opens?'

'We'll have to hunt for a parachute,' said Vosper with a bark of laughter.

Paul decided to concentrate on the purpose of their mission. Aerial views of the English countryside could usually reveal more than land views about ancient paths and boundaries, they could pick out changes in soil and development. In this case the theory was that they might pick out evidence of a recent walk across the fields, by someone carrying a heavy body over his shoulder when it was too dark to worry about paths. At the very least they should find some fragments of clothing once they had established the route.

'Supposing,' Paul said perversely, 'it was Ronnie Kelby. He wouldn't have taken the body across the fields. He would have gone the long way round in his father's car.'

'Maybe, but we've checked the car and it tells us nothing.'

They hovered over Melford House. Two policemen and a dog climbed out of a car in the road, waved in acknowledgment and then set off down the road. A hundred yards along they turned left through a swing gate into the potato field. PC Anderson was talking to them through a walkie-talkie.

'I've been thinking about Ronnie Kelby's alibi,' said Paul. 'He needn't have put the body in the rain butt on Monday evening.'

'Are you trying to be helpful?' Vosper growled.

'Anybody could have put it there at five o'clock on Tuesday morning.'

'Why don't you concentrate on feeling nervous, Temple?'

Over the brow of the hill the crops changed to corn for nearly half a mile, then to the cow pasture which Mortimer owned. There was a stile between the potatoes and the corn field. The dog appeared to scent a rabbit at that point and it scurried off into the hedgerow, but the policemen had found something by the stile itself. They waved up to the helicopter.

'What have they found?' Charlie Vosper asked the policeman next to him.

'It's a note.' The man sounded excited. 'A note from Mr Kelby.'

'Saying what?'

The policeman consulted his colleagues on the ground, and gradually the writing on the wet piece of paper was deciphered.

'It's from Mr Kelby and it says:

"Of course I'll meet you if it's so important. But it had better not be at the house. You know how things have changed. Can we meet at the stile where we used to meet? Say ten o'clock this evening. Yours ever, Alfred."'

Charlie Vosper muttered to himself while he assimilated the new information, then he told the men to continue the search.

'You'll never believe this,' Paul said delightedly, 'but I said to Steve this morning that we need a woman in the case.'

'I believe you.'

'Did Kelby have a girlfriend these last few months?' Paul asked the inspector.

'No, at least not since Ronnie came home. Nobody's mentioned a girl except you.' Charlie Vosper snorted grimly. 'And the girl you described sounded like one of his students.'

'No, not necessarily.' She had impressed Paul as a sexy little thing with lots of animal vitality. Paul had wondered then how Kelby stood the pace. But of course she could have been an intellectual with it. 'She was young, that was all.'

Instead of returning to the field headquarters they went round to the local police station. It was really a house that dated from the days when a village bobby had lived there. But the police had expanded since then, and the small local force used all eight rooms as offices and kept the basement as a lockup for the occasional drunk. They found Inspector Hobden in the erstwhile parlour.

'We need your help,' said Vosper. 'After all, you've known these people since they were so high. Local man.' Vosper sat before the unnecessary coal fire and beamed encouragingly. 'Tell me the gossip on Kelby. Did he have girlfriends? Who were they? What were his sexual habits?'

Hobden fidgeted uncomfortably. 'I don't think he had a girlfriend these last couple of years. At least, not in Melford.'

'Two years ago?'

'Well, there was a girl, according to rumour. But she left Melford and went off to college somewhere.'

Charlie Vosper nodded. 'So what was the situation then? Was there a scandal?'

'I'm a policeman, Inspector Vosper, not a village barman. How would I know about Kelby's sex life? If he had a sex

46

life he was discreet about it, and his friends haven't told me about the old scandals before I came.'

'Before you came?'

'I've only been responsible for this division for eighteen months. I came out from Oxford.'

They left the police station in disgust. 'Back to the routine enquiries,' Charlie Vosper complained. 'We don't get any short cuts from the local men. What the devil happened to village life?'

Paul telephoned Steve to say that he was coming home. Maybe they could have lunch together. Or had she eaten?

'No,' she said excitedly, 'I've been trying to contact you. Did you see the obituaries in the paper this morning?'

'Yes, of course—'

'Sir Philip Tranmere is dead! Don't you remember? He was the man who telephoned Lady Delamore yesterday. I told you about him.'

Paul remembered.

'He committed suicide last night.'

Paul went off and bought another copy of *The Times*. It was tucked away at the foot of the column. Sir Philip Tranmere. The small photograph showed a flushed port-drinking face with military moustache and baggy eyes. He probably barked when he spoke and thought the country had gone to the dogs. But his distinguished military career had ended abruptly in 1947 when he had been arrested on suspicion of murdering Lord Delamore at a shooting party in Scotland. Some days later he had been released for lack of evidence, but that had been the end of his career.

So much for a domestic lunch with Steve.

Chapter 6

THE body of Sir Philip Tranmere was in the morgue, but it explained nothing. Sir Philip had jumped out of the window at his club shortly after midnight – a hundred feet onto the pavement.

'It's really most irregular, sir,' the club secretary repeated three times. 'We don't expect our members to do things like this here. The last time it happened was in 1892.'

The secretary was more like a bank manager.

'I didn't know much about Sir Philip. He was a member before I took over. He always behaved himself, did the right thing.' He sighed. 'He was rather a lonely old boy, but so are many of our members. I gather he lived in a service flat in St John's Wood. Came in three or four times a week. He can't have lived much of a life. Nothing much to look forward to.'

'He had a few things to look back on,' said Paul. 'Did he seem worried these last few days?'

'We always took the view that the past was a long time ago,' the secretary said reprovingly. 'And Sir Philip was a gentleman. If he were worried he would not have confided in the barman.'

Paul thanked him breezily and went through into the lounge. It was nearly empty. There was a man in a well-cut, blue-grey suit standing three feet back from the barman.

'What I always say is,' he was declaiming uncertainly, 'that if you're still alive you haven't much to complain about.'

The barman was not in philosophic mood. 'We're closing now.' He picked up the bowler hat from his counter and tossed it to the customer. The elderly clubmen were not given the service they had been accustomed to. Although this elderly clubman was in his late forties. Paul took the hint and left. He paid an unofficial visit to a friend just down the road in Whitehall.

'I'm not talking to you, Temple.'

Paul sat comfortably in the leather armchair and relaxed. He stared around him at the oak panelling and the wall-to-wall carpet. Harry had a nice panoramic view of London from his window. He had got on since the days when he had been the youngest superintendent in the police force.

'Why?' asked Paul. 'Is this room bugged?'

'You used that information I gave you about the PPS to the Secretary of Defence. You used it in a novel. I recognised the plot.'

'Come off it, Harry, you can't even read.'

'I don't need to. I'm telepathic. You've come here to ask me about Sir Philip Tranmere.'

Paul grinned. 'You must have seen the picture in *The Times* this morning.'

Harry had been in charge of the investigation into Lord Delamore's death in 1947. Not that Paul had known him in those days. Paul had been commissioned to do a series of colour supplement articles on real-life detectives some years ago and had met Harry then. The difficulty had been that nearly all of Harry's exploits, accurately reported, would have earned him an early retirement. The police force had taken the more sensible course of promoting him out of harm's way.

'Have a glass of port,' said Harry.

One thing about Harry's elevated position, it didn't seem to entail any work. The man just wandered about being unpleasant to everybody, bawling out his staff and terrorising criminals, and everybody loved him. He created the illusion that underneath his misanthropic waistcoat (or vest, as he called it) throbbed a human being. It was an illusion.

Harry unlocked the false front to the bookcase and produced the drinks. He poured a substantial whisky and soda for himself, and offered Paul the decanter.

'I'm cutting down on the whisky,' he said as he closed the bookcase. 'That's why I keep it locked. Last week I told the Home Secretary that he wouldn't even qualify as a filing clerk in my office. Secretary? He can't even type. I wasn't wrong, Paul, the man's an idiot. But I said that at three o'clock in the afternoon. Too much whisky. I don't normally say things like that to ministers until after eight. So I'm cutting down.'

He raised the glass in salute.

'Now, what's this I've been hearing about a diary? My Inspector Vosper says it's missing.'

Paul nodded. 'Someone murdered Alfred Kelby to get hold of it.'

'And Rover Tranmere has committed suicide. Well?'

'I wondered what went on at the shooting lodge in 1947.'

'God knows,' said Harry with a laugh. 'There were about fifteen people staying there, including the secretary and a couple of servants, and they were suffering from what we used to call the three As. Affluence, adultery and alcohol. It was a hot summer and I suppose they ran out of grouse. From sheer boredom probably they began shooting each other. They were a shabby, quarrelsome crew. Perhaps I was young and impressionable then, but what surprised me was that with so much jumping in and out of each other's beds they should all dislike each other so much. It seemed inconsistent.'

Lord Delamore had assembled a party of rich or fashionable people. Kelby, who had published a life of Hitler that year, Tranmere, who had been in the news for killing natives in Malaya, an up-and-coming politician, an actor who was off to Hollywood. The Delamores knew how to compile a guest list. They had made up the number, after the lesser diplomat, the stockbroker and the motorcar tycoon, with a trio of models elegant in the year's 'New Look'.

'Lord Delamore acted as a kind of ringmaster, organising the revels to create the maximum drama and embarrassment,' said Harry. 'After a week somebody shot him. It could have been any one of them, but finding out exactly who made solving Chinese puzzles look easy. They all lied about where they had been at two o'clock that morning, or who they had been with, and half of them were too drunk to remember. You should have seen what the newspapers made of it!'

'Why did you arrest Sir Philip Tranmere?' Paul asked.

'I thought he'd done it. He hated Lord Delamore and he was Lady Delamore's lover. But there was no evidence. He couldn't remember whether he'd done it or not.'

'Poor old Tranmere,' Paul murmured.

'I don't mind a man who takes a drink occasionally,' said Harry with an air of tolerance. 'But I can't stand a fellow who falls over.'

'Do you know who did kill him?' Paul asked.

'No. It was one of those cases I was almost glad not to solve. There would have been even more lurid journalism

51

at the trial. I was relieved to let the whole affair die down. There was more pressing work to do.'

Paul spent the next few hours mugging up his post-war social history in the classical mausoleum of Kensington Central Library, going through back numbers of *The Times* and looking up what he could of the popular Sunday newspapers. It had been a grim period, and the public had clearly enjoyed the light relief which the scandal had provided. It had been the time of *Forever Amber* and *The Outlaw*, when lush escapism was needed.

When Paul reached home at eight o'clock he found that Scott Reed was there waiting. And Steve had already scared him with her premonition of death.

'Who'd want to kill me?' he asked plaintively. 'I'm only a simple publisher.'

Kate Balfour had spent two days preparing l'Estouffat de Boeuf and she served it up with apologies that it was really a farmhouse dish, not quite suited to twentieth-century kitchens. It was soaked in wine and the sauce tasted like pure Armagnac. By the end of the meal even Scott Reed was relaxed. He was spearing pieces of Caerphilly without seeing his own stomach beneath the knife.

He was even inclined to be metaphysical about death. 'I'm not afraid,' he said over the brandy. 'I could do with the rest.' He was nodding solemnly to himself as he changed his mind. 'It's a rather positive thing, though, rather irreversible. You can't change your mind once you've been killed, can you?' He lit a cigar and coughed. 'I suppose you think I'm in danger because of the diary?'

Steve explained that it had seemed like a probability. 'But I expect Paul has it worked out.'

'Who else has read the diary?' Paul intervened, 'apart from Kelby?'

'Nobody. Apart from me. And Bella Spender. I doubt whether Kelby had time to read it, because he disappeared half an hour after I left the diary with him.'

'Perhaps the killer couldn't take a chance on that,' said Paul.

Scott Reed moved cautiously away from the window. 'We'd better get to the bottom of this, hadn't we?'

Paul Temple agreed. 'Who did the diary say killed Lord Tranmere?'

'Some minor diplomatic type called Price-Pemberton. I've never heard of him. But the diary wouldn't be evidence, would it? I mean, he wouldn't need to worry about being convicted.'

'No,' Paul said with a laugh, 'but I doubt whether you would persuade him to sign your release. He might even sue you.'

He went to the *Who's Who* on his bookshelves, but Price-Pemberton was not entered. He wasn't in the London telephone directory either.

'Do you think,' Steve asked him, 'that Price-Pemberton will be jumping out of the windows of his club?'

'It's an idea,' said Paul.

He telephoned Lady Delamore. It was a difficult conversation, because she claimed not to know Price-Pemberton and then, having remembered, affected not to have kept in touch. 'Little Willy was rather tiresome,' she shrilled down the telephone. 'Always wanted women older than himself. I was very relieved when he gave up the diplomatic service and dropped out of my own life. That was when I invented the phrase: 'Dead, dead, and never called me mother'. He would never have made an ambassador.'

'Is he dead then?' Paul asked.

'No. It's a quotation from *East Lynne*. Not my favourite book. Willy retired and went to live on the Thames, somewhere near Marlow. But of course he might have drowned in the last twenty-five years.'

Paul agreed and hung up feeling not much wiser.

'Scott,' he said wearily, 'I suppose you'll go through with the business of asking everybody named in the diary to sign a release?'

'Is it worth doing now?'

'I don't know. You might get some interesting reactions.' He poured himself another brandy. 'I suppose you hadn't got round to approaching Sir Philip Tranmere?'

Scott leaned forward in the egg-shaped chair. 'It's funny you should ask that, because I bumped into him the night before last. I met him at my club, just by chance, and he said he would sign. He didn't seem very interested.'

'How funny,' Paul murmured. 'Perhaps after all you had better not approach any of the others.'

'I've no idea where to find most of them. A lot of debutantes and models who are probably living in Australia, and of course some of them have died quite naturally. I was going to put an ad in the personal column of *The Times*. And then there are some policemen . . .'

'Policemen never commit suicide,' Steve pronounced.

Paul walked thoughtfully to the window and stared across the Thames. 'Speaking of debutantes,' he said, 'who was that girl I used to see with Kelby? She was an attractive young thing.'

'Oh, Jennie. She was his girlfriend.'

'Jennie?' Paul opened a window to clear his mind of tobacco smoke and brandy. 'Tell me more. What did she do?'

'She took off all her clothes at a party I gave to launch Kelby's history of the Spanish civil war. It was nearly midnight, but my wife was still there and she was appalled.

54

Kelby didn't seem to notice. He was arguing with one of those left-wing poets. She had a beautiful figure.'

'What happened to her?'

'I don't know. Perhaps she married a nice young man and settled down. Although I pity the nice young man.'

It might have been his imagination, or else Paul had seen a shadow move down in the mews doorway opposite. It looked like a man standing back in the darkest corner.

'My goodness,' said Scott as the sound of the church clock on the other side of Battersea Park came clearly across the water. It was striking eleven. 'Is that the time? My wife will think I've been killed.' The inappositeness of his little joke suddenly occurred to him and he giggled unhappily. 'You know what my wife is like.'

'Hang on a moment,' said Paul.

He went through to the kitchen where Kate was finishing the washing up. Paul told her that he and Steve would attend to that.

It was ten minutes past eleven when Scott Reed left the house. Paul watched him from the upstairs window. Scott climbed into his Rover 2000 and while the car door was open the interior light clearly showed a man sitting in the passenger seat. He appeared to say something, and then the car drove off towards the Albert Bridge.

Chapter 7

KATE BALFOUR was not the most efficient housekeeper in the world. She tried hard, and some of her cooking was out of this century. But she often found better things to do with her time than housework, and her treatment of Paul's visitors was occasionally deplorable. Only the previous month she had thrown a guest down the stairs and broken three of his ribs. The police force had never been a very good training ground for domestic service.

She followed Scott Reed out of London and on to the Portsmouth Road in Paul's Jaguar. Scott Reed lived in Hambledon, just the other side of Godalming, and if the mystery passenger was going all the way with him then she didn't have much to worry about; until she reached Hambledon. She cruised down at seventy miles an hour, about twenty-five seconds behind the Rover. She calculated that if they stopped in front of her she would know it soon enough.

Her initial reaction had been to curse Scott Reed for not living in Islington like every other publisher. Hambledon after all was a two-hour drive into Surrey! But once past Surbiton her stout policewoman's heart was gradu- ally uplifted by the countryside. The silver birches looked elegantly sparse in the full moonlight. The huge cliffs of sandstone that frequently towered on either side of the road were deceptively majestic.

From time to time on the deserted road she glimpsed the Rover ahead; its tail lights blinked whenever Scott Reed braked and sometimes she saw the car and its two passengers silhouetted on the crest of a hill. Going down the steep slope that was Guildford she nearly ran into the back of them. They seemed to be chatting amiably.

A few minutes later Kate was manoeuvring the narrow, ancient streets of Godalming and she felt again the tranquil atmosphere of the early nineteenth century. That was when she lost the car in front.

She increased speed, hoping to reach Scott Reed's house before disaster befell him. And to hell with discreet tailing! She hit eighty through the rural wastes of Witley and then slowed down at the top of the hill: Scott Reed lived somewhere over to the left. She glanced at an impressive building on her right – a charity board school of some kind that didn't know its place. And then the turning on the left just by the pig farm. Kate did a racing driver's turn, alongside Hambledon Common and round to the stockbrokers' Tudor residence of Scott Reed.

Scott Reed and the mystery man were just letting themselves into the house.

Kate left the Jaguar on the other side of the green and walked back to the house. She noted approvingly that the high walls and massive gates were a sufficient deterrent to casual crime. But determined burglars or ex-policewomen can manage these things. She shinned over the wall with an agility that rendered her fifteen stone ridiculous and crept up to the windows.

She saw Scott Reed in his living room pouring drinks from his cupboard for the stranger. It was impossible to hear what they were saying, but they appeared to be on friendly terms. She noted the stranger's appearance: medium build, five feet eight, dark hair and swarthy complexion, aged forty to fifty, no distinguishing features. A crook.

Kate had noticed a telephone booth two hundred yards back along the road, outside a general store-cum-post office. She slipped away to make a call.

'That was Kate,' said Paul as he tossed his silk dressing gown onto the bed. 'She's down in Hambledon.'

Steve grunted.

'The mystery visitor is down there with Scott, drinking and chatting like an old friend.'

'Well, there you are,' she mumbled meaninglessly.

'I wonder how he means to get back to London.'

'Darling, come to bed. Your feet will get cold again, and you know I hate that. Kate can look after herself.'

Paul slipped into bed, brushing a cold foot against Steve as he did so. 'Poor Kate. I don't really think you like her.'

'She's an absolute treasure, I know all about that, but I always expect her to break into a quick chorus of "Proceeding in a Westerly Direction" as she plugs in the vacuum cleaner. Do you think cold feet should rate as a ground for divorce? And anyway it's rather an affectation to employ an ex-policewoman as a domestic help.'

Paul turned out the bedside lamp and snuggled up to her warm body. 'We pay her more than she earned as a WPC,' he murmured.

'Shut up and say something romantic.'

Kate shuddered as she walked back to the village green. It was cold in the country. A few stray wisps of cloud were streaming across the face of the moon, but it was a cold night. The stars flickered icily. She thanked God for making her fat, though she called it generous, and leaped to one side as a maniac bore down on her in a fast car.

'Maniac!' she shouted angrily.

She memorised the registration number as a conditioned reflex, it was her police training. Three seconds later she spun round and shouted again. 'Hey, come back!' It was Mr Temple's Jaguar! But it was out of sight and on its way back to London.

That morning Steve cooked the breakfast and burnt the toast. 'I'm worried about Kate,' she explained. 'Did you see that the car is down in the mews? I do hope nothing has happened to her!'

'Hypocrite,' Paul laughed.

'You know the kind of man we're dealing with,' Steve said heatedly. 'She may be dead!'

'I've already looked in the boot. It was empty.'

'Who was that man she described?'

Paul sighed. 'It could have been anybody.' He bit carefully into the toast and chewed thoroughly. 'You know what police descriptions are like: medium build, dark complexion, everybody I know fits Kate's description, except a few women. This toast is well done, isn't it?'

'I think you should ring up Scott Reed.'

It was nice to see her slightly agitated first thing in the morning. Paul had been brought up on the myth that women looked like something else in the morning. Hair curlers and face cream, flesh unaccountably in the wrong places. As if women were assembled between eight o'clock and noon. But Steve was tiresomely neat and Steve as soon as she woke up. It was nice to see that she was less than perfect.

'What did you do with this coffee?' he asked provocatively. 'It tastes as if you made it with tea.'

'Darling, instead of being terribly witty, shouldn't you be finding out what has happened to that poor woman?'

He telephoned Scott Reed. It might sound a little odd, saying please can I have my cook back, but Scott had to know something of her whereabouts. And he sounded evasive, which confirmed Paul's feeling.

'No, I reached home safely,' Scott assured him. 'But it's thoughtful of you to worry.' There was a pause, during which Paul could envisage the publisher changing his mind and worrying and reversing his decisions. 'As a matter of fact I bumped into an old friend when I left you, so nothing could have happened to me. He came all the way back to Hambledon.'

'Who,' Paul asked, trying to sound casual, 'was that?'

'Arthur Grover. He lives in one of the big houses here. Rather a dubious character, actually, we've always assumed he was a bit of a gangster. But last night I was glad about that, because Arthur thought we were being followed. I tell you, Paul, I'm rather jumpy.'

'You were being followed,' said Paul. 'Kate Balfour trailed you down there. And now she's missing.'

'Kate? Missing?' There was another pause. 'Arthur wouldn't have . . . It's only our joke, over in the pub, about him being a gangster. Perhaps I should have a word with him.'

Paul Temple spent an hour or so checking on Mr Arthur Grover. It was a name that sounded familiar, and Paul prided himself on knowing most of the gangsters in London and the south east. But somehow it was a name he associated with America. Las Vegas. What was a man who belonged on the American club circuit doing in Surrey?

'I fancy a quick drink before lunch,' said Paul. 'Are you coming down to the corner?'

Steve looked aghast. 'You've only just had breakfast. Isn't this a little early for quick drinks?'

'I'll make it a tomato juice.'

'There's some in the fridge—'

The pub on the corner was crowded, but with the best people. No petty criminals or amateur prostitutes. Strictly the better class of criminals and showbiz people, rich business men with expensive girls. It was the best place outside Soho to keep in touch with what was happening, and Eric was a useful barman. More, he was a friend.

Paul nodded amiably to a couple of plain-clothes detectives alone in the corner of the bar. They were also keeping in touch. It was better than pounding the pavements.

'Hello, Mr Temple,' said Eric as they reached the bar. 'I didn't know you were back from the States.'

'I arrived back on Wednesday. What shall we have, Steve?'

'A martini for me,' she said sweetly, 'and you were going to have a tomato juice.' She leaned across for the Worcester sauce. Even the most trendy of pubs were, in her opinion, for men.

'I'm trying to find out something about a man called Arthur Grover,' Paul said when the drinks came. 'Have you heard of him?'

'Arthur? Yes, of course. What's he been up to?'

'I wish I knew. Who is he?'

'Arthur? He runs the Casino Club in Reigate Street. Runs it with Neville the Nob. I thought you met him in Las Vegas—'

It all clicked into place. Paul could almost see the face.

He had met Arthur Grover briefly about three years ago. There had been some confusion over their seats, and while

61

the management sorted it out Paul and Arthur Grover had done the English thing and had a drink together. Mr Grover had given the impression that he was a club tycoon over there to study American methods.

'What does he look like?' Paul asked.

'Well,' said Eric, 'medium build, dark complexion—'

'Oh shut up.' Paul laughed. 'Is he straight?'

'Good lord no!'

Steve was listening in blank disbelief. 'I don't believe it,' she said. 'If this man Grover is behind the theft of the diary and a murder then Scott Reed must be implicated as well. And I don't believe Scott would go to all the trouble of bringing Kelby into it when he could simply have handed over the diary in a Hambledon pub. Anyway, Scott is quite incapable of deception. He's the sort of person who would be found out if he forgot to pay his fare on the bus. Why would he harm Kate?'

'I think we need answers to all those points,' said Paul. 'Eric, can I make a phone call?'

Paul looked up the telephone number and then rang the Casino Club. It was difficult to persuade them to put him through to Grover, until he mentioned the name of Temple. Then Arthur Grover was on the line instantly.

'I had the pleasure of meeting you three years back,' said Paul. 'In Las Vegas. Dean Martin was doing the floor show.'

Arthur Grover sounded cautious. He muttered something non-committal about Dean being a great little artiste. He sounded as if he were talking round a cigar, and there was the trace of an American accent.

'I wanted to thank you for returning my car this morning,' said Paul. 'I would have been sorry to lose that Jaguar. But I wondered when I could expect my cook to be returned.'

'Your cook?'

'She followed you back with Scott Reed last night.' A sudden edge entered Paul's voice, an edge of menace. 'I get hungry when I don't eat, Grover, and then I get vicious. Now, are we going to be civilised and have a talk together?'

'I don't know what you're talking about,' he began. But then he thought better of argument. 'I'll see you at Scott's home this afternoon. I want to talk to you anyway.'

The A3 was a strange road, especially since the Guildford bypass had changed everything and traffic drifted automatically out to Hindhead and towards Petersfield. In that part of the country Paul always fell into reveries about Freeman Wills Crofts, and he ended up theorising about the art of the whodunnit, then he missed the road to Chiddingfold. Paul tried to think about his serious study of death. Out there to the right Mike Hawthorne had been killed, and farther on a sailor had been hanged near Hindhead. Violent deaths. Gratuitous even.

He looked at the countryside instead. That had a pattern, a seasonal repetition. The gorse and bracken were much the same as they must have been a million years ago. The gorse grey and lying across the ground like wire at this time of the year, ferns green and not yet tall, weak and succulent. They were the only plants that could thrive unaided in the Surrey sand. And now, a million years later, the ferns still made excellent spears for small boys to throw at each other.

Paul arrived in Hambledon at half past three.

Arthur Grover turned out to be a sleek, sinister character with a lot of bustling energy and a cigar-waving self-confidence. Paul remembered him as soon as he saw him. He was not a man who would be easy to intimidate. But he shook hands with Paul and growled hello.

They went through into Scott's living room, where the publisher was serving tea. It was not a scene into which Soho mobsters fitted easily. Paul sat by the window and waited while the tea cups were handed round. The view from the window was a grey-green expanse of common rising to the convent school on the hill.

'I'm sorry, Paul,' Scott Reed began nervously. 'I should have told you when you telephoned this morning. But I didn't know what to say.'

'Why, what happened?'

'Mr Grover was waiting for me when I left you last night.'

Paul turned to Arthur Grover. 'I think you might as well do the talking.'

Arthur Grover bit into a small sandwich while he considered. 'I wanted to know what was going on. I read in the papers about Kelby being dead, and I wanted to know what had happened. You see, I stole the diary from Kelby, but I didn't kill him.'

Paul nodded. That made sense. 'I always said that Scott Reed ought not to be allowed to mix with the real world. There are too many people like you about, and Scott gets himself into trouble.'

'What do you mean?' Scott blustered. 'Mr Grover is a neighbour. You don't even know what happened, Paul.'

'I can guess. I expect you talked to Mr Grover in the saloon bar one evening, over there in the pub on the green where you both play the game of country squires. You probably told him about this extraordinary diary that you meant to publish.'

'I may have done—'

'You wouldn't have known that Neville Delamore was the respectable half of the Grover–Delamore partnership who own the Casino Club in Reigate Street, the English half.' Paul Temple smiled at Grover. 'Arthur Grover is an American, so he has to have a respectable front man to satisfy the Gaming Board. Has he never boasted to you of his aristocratic friends?'

Grover glowered round his cigar. 'Are you threatening me?'

'Not at all, but you are slightly vulnerable, Mr Grover. You know how nervous we are in this country of our gambling clubs being controlled by outsiders. I suppose if Neville Delamore needed a diary retrieving to preserve his family name you could scarcely refuse.'

'He's a bit of a snob like that,' said Grover, 'and he didn't want his mother to be hurt. But Neville's a good boy. He didn't ask me any favours. I said I'd get the diary back.'

Paul shrugged. 'Just like that.'

'Yes, just like that,' he said, angrily stubbing out his cigar. 'I have the manpower. It was no trouble. On Monday morning a gang of us went out to Melford Cross and picked up Kelby. The intention was to hold him until his secretary handed over the diary. But to our surprise we found that wasn't necessary.'

'Because,' Paul prompted, 'Kelby had the diary on him when you picked him up.'

'Right, Mr Temple. Unfortunately the old boy guessed what we were up to; there was a struggle and he was knocked unconscious. Some of my men are over-excitable, and I had to speak to Bates afterwards. Later that day, after Kelby had recovered, we left him in the shed at the bottom of his garden.'

'Go on,' said Paul.

'I telephoned the house and told Ronnie Kelby his father was safe, and that he'd find him in the gardener's shed.'

Paul was thoughtful. 'You spoke to Ronnie Kelby yourself?'

'I did indeed.'

Paul turned to the nervous publisher, who was nodding enthusiastically. 'That's it, Paul, that's what Mr Grover told me last night. I said he should tell you the whole truth. He didn't murder anybody.' He glanced nervously at Grover. 'At least, that was what he told me.'

'Of course I didn't murder Kelby. I stole the diary, that's all.'

'And gave it to Neville Delamore?'

'Right.'

'And what about Kate Balfour? What did you do with her?'

Arthur Grover sighed irritably. 'What would you do if you found someone on your tail? I put the boys onto her to find out who the hell she was. Since then she's been up at my house, waiting for the outcome of our little discussion.' He lit another cigar. 'So what is the outcome?'

'I believe you, but I can't guarantee the police won't take action against you for stealing the diary, or whatever charge they might come up with after the case is cleared up. And I can't guarantee that your gambling licence will be renewed.'

Paul saw the sturdy figure of Kate Balfour striding across the common towards the house. She looked forbiddingly fit and purposive. A few hours' detention never harmed a police-woman. Paul grinned at the sight. He felt slightly sorry for the man who had been her gaoler. He went to the door to meet her.

'But,' he called back to Arthur Grover, 'I'll tell Inspector Vosper you play by the rules. He likes that in a crook.'

Paul held open the door of the Jaguar to Kate and kissed her on the cheek. She smiled sheepishly and sat in the passenger seat.

'I'm sorry, Paul,' she said as they drove back. 'I didn't realise he would have a gang at his disposal.'

Paul laughed. 'Don't apologise. You did a splendid job, Kate, and I'm grateful.'

'Immediately after he drove off in your Jaguar four men leaped on me.'

'That only goes to show you are as young as you feel.'

She smiled severely. 'Did we get anywhere today, as a result?'

'I think we did, Kate. We discovered the case is more complicated than it might have been. But that's not your fault.'

He swung out onto the Guildford bypass and increased speed to seventy miles an hour. It seemed a great pity to whizz through the Surrey countryside without looking at it again. But there were more pressing things than nature for the moment. For one thing Paul was hungry.

Chapter 8

THE missing blonde appeared on Saturday.

Kelby was being buried in the village churchyard at Melford Cross. It had been discreetly arranged by Tracy Leonard, to avoid the kind of spectacular which Kelby would have found distasteful. No ghouls or rubbernecks, simply a few close friends, the family, and Detective Inspector Charlie Vosper. Some thirty-five people filed out of the tiny fourteenth-century church and followed the coffin to the graveside.

'So Neville Chamberlain will have to wait a few more years,' a distinguished historian murmured to Paul Temple. 'There aren't many of us with Kelby's moral courage.'

Paul watched the strangely formal ritual of lowering the coffin, inaudible prayers swept away on the April winds, the scattering of the first handfuls of earth onto the box. Kelby's death was wantonly unnecessary, Paul reflected; at least when the Duke of Clarence was drowned in a vat of malmsey the English throne was at stake.

Tracy Leonard was wiping away a single tear. She looked classical in her grief, tall like Electra and dressed in black. Whereas Ronnie Kelby was flushed and furious, as if he thought that his father had let him down again. At the end of the ceremony he turned swiftly away and strode towards the wrought-iron gates.

There was another woman in mourning standing separate from the main congregation. She was the blonde, and the black dress, the veil across her face, made her look alabaster white. It seemed as if everybody else at the funeral knew who she was, Paul sensed, because they pointedly ignored her. She was a source of embarrassment.

Leo and Gladys were looking out of place, lurking among the people by the graveside as if they had no right to be there, servants among the gentry. When most other people had gone and the gravedigger began filling in the grave Leo Ashwood remained staring. The blonde in black smiled at Leo as she left, but he stared bleakly through her. He didn't move until the coffin had been completely covered, and then he left without a word.

Paul caught up with the blonde and fell into step beside her. 'Good morning. We've met before, at Scott Reed's New Year party. I'm Paul Temple. I'm sorry we meet again under such unhappy circumstances.'

'So am I,' she said without much interest. Her voice was soft, and all trace of a regional accent had been diligently removed. 'I remember you. You're a detective novelist. I read one of your books after that party. It didn't have much sex in it.'

Paul was taken aback. 'Did you guess who did it?' he asked helplessly.

'No. I still didn't know when I finished the book.'

Paul had a feeling he had been outpointed. 'I understand you used to live in Melford.'

'Of course.' She turned with a radiantly artificial smile. 'And how nice it is to be back home!'

They had reached the gates of the cemetery. Detective Inspector Vosper was standing there waiting beside his police car. 'Hello, Jennie,' he said, opening the police car door. Jennie got into the car without a murmur. The waft of her scent remained in the air to remind Paul she had been beside him.

'Well, Temple,' said Charlie Vosper, 'did you find the missing diary?'

'No, although I discovered who stole it,' said Paul. 'I'm beginning to agree with you. It has no bearing on the case.' He flinched as the inspector slammed his car door. 'You haven't made any arrests yet?'

'I want to know about that diary. If you hold anything back from me—'

'Charlie,' Paul laughed, 'you've had a change of heart! I thought you told me the diary was irrelevant?'

'That was before I was summoned to the assistant commissioner's office. I've been warned off, Temple, told to lay off the official history side.' Vosper forced his craggy features into an unconvincing smile. 'This is the first time I've ever been thankful to have you around on a case, Paul. It means you can tell me what I'm not allowed to know.'

'But there's nothing—'

'When my assistant commissioner tells me to mind my own business, I know there's something going on that's very much my business. I'll see you in a couple of hours.' He glanced at his watch and then at the pub across from the war memorial. 'I'll see you in that pub at seven o'clock.'

Vosper climbed quickly into the car beside Jennie and waved to the driver.

'Wait a minute. Charlie! What was the autopsy report on Kelby?'

The inspector wound down his window. 'Kelby was strangled, died of a broken neck. There wasn't a drop of water in his lungs.' The car swung round and headed rapidly towards London.

Paul waited by his Jaguar as Leo and Gladys Ashwood came from the churchyard, and as they passed he offered them a lift. 'It's a bleak day to walk all that way,' he said kindly. Gladys accepted.

'It was a nice service,' she said contentedly. 'It was nice to see all those friends of Mr Kelby turn out.'

'I'm glad you're feeling better,' said Paul.

'I like funerals,' she explained. 'They make it seem somehow all right. Not that we aren't upset any more, but a funeral is something you can come to grips with.'

'I know what you mean.'

Leo had said not a word, and in the driving mirror Paul saw him smile slightly at his wife's efforts to put her feelings into words.

'Who was the dramatic-looking blonde?' Paul asked. 'Everyone seemed to know her.'

'Who was that?' asked Leo.

'She smiled at you as she left. The girl I was talking to. She just drove off with Inspector Vosper.'

Leo grunted. 'She used to live in the area, but she's left now.' They drove on in silence.

'We're not having a farewell party,' Gladys Ashwood explained as they reached the house. 'It wouldn't be right, not after the way he died. With his murderer still not caught. But please come in, Mr Temple. I'll be making some tea in a moment. Miss Leonard and Master Ronnie will be in the living room somewhere.'

'That's very kind.'

Paul went through the kitchen and into the hall. He found them in the library. Tracy Leonard was half-heartedly

71

collecting up some papers from various corners of the room and putting them in order. Ronnie was helplessly watching her. There was nothing to do, but Tracy was trying in a desultory way to keep herself occupied. Paul noticed that on closer inspection she was looking drawn. The death and the sleeping pills were combining to make her haggard.

'Sure, come in,' said Ronnie. 'I saw you arrive.'

'I know this is not the time to intrude—'

Ronnie broke in impatiently. 'That's all right. Anything that will help to solve this damned mystery.'

'Even,' Tracy murmured ironically, 'you, Mr Temple.'

The two of them were functioning as a team now, the hostility Paul had sensed earlier was gone. It was the effect of adversity shared, Paul assumed, like a population at war. Ronnie could recognise a woman to lean on when he saw one.

Paul smiled at her irony. 'I'd like to help, but I know even less about the case than Inspector Vosper does, I'm afraid.'

'That's impossible.' Miss Leonard adopted the tone she used on the unfortunate policeman. 'He's been padding about here all the week asking fatuous questions about our movements and getting nowhere. The man's a fool. Obviously our movements don't help in the slightest. We didn't know there was going to be a murder, so none of us has an alibi. We didn't know it would be necessary to have one.'

'Poor old Charlie Vosper,' Paul said gently. 'He has to fill in the details. It helps to know, for instance, that Mr Kelby left for a meeting in the village at eleven thirty. Then he had an appointment for half past four with Ted Mortimer, which apparently he never kept. We know where he was at half past four. But he also had an assignment with a woman for ten o'clock that night, and we've no idea whether he kept that assignment.'

'What woman was this?' Ronnie asked in astonishment.

'I don't know.' Tracy Leonard had turned sickly pale. 'Do you know who it might have been, Miss Leonard?'

She shook her head. 'No, I'm afraid— no. It must be a mistake.' She was thrown off balance.

'Who could it have been, Miss Leonard?'

'Why should I know? I'm his secretary. Mr Kelby's personal habits were no concern of mine. If he made assignments, as you call them, they would be his private affair.'

'Did he have a mistress, Miss Leonard, either now or in the past five years?'

'Probably.' She glared at him. 'Even the most brilliant men have their feet of clay. But they don't usually ask their secretaries to make the arrangements!'

Paul smiled understandingly. 'It helps to know what Kelby was doing that day. And obviously it helps to know what other people were doing at the same time. What were you doing, for instance, Ronnie?'

'Me?' He was surprised by the question. 'I don't know. I've already told you and the inspector. I just messed about. I was late getting up.' He shrugged nervously. 'I took things easy. After lunch I went down to the club and had a game of golf.'

'And in the evening?'

'Well, most of the evening Tracy and I were driving around trying to find out what had happened to my father. About ten o'clock we decided we were getting nowhere so we went over to the police station.'

Paul nodded encouragingly. 'Was that before or after the phone call?'

'Phone call?' He was startled, and he glanced in alarm towards Tracy. 'I don't know. What phone call?'

'Didn't someone telephone on Monday evening?'

'No, I've already told you. No one telephoned me. Tracy and I were together the whole evening! If I'd received a phone call she would have known about it.'

Paul looked enquiringly at Tracy Leonard. She shook her head in confirmation.

'We were together all evening.' She took the tray of tea and buttered crumpets from Gladys Ashwood and began serving. 'Wouldn't it be more sensible to assume that Mr Kelby was murdered by someone who wished to get his hands on that diary, Mr Temple?'

'It would be more simple,' Paul agreed. 'It would clear you and Ronnie and everyone else here of suspicion. It would be more convenient for you.'

She smiled. 'You speak as if that were reprehensible. But for myself I would like to be cleared of suspicion.'

Paul agreed good-humouredly that everyone hoped she would be. He was beginning to understand why Charlie Vosper was a misanthrope. He tried to direct the questions back to Ronnie Kelby. He nibbled some buttered toast and said conversationally that he too had just come back from the United States. Such an exciting country, such friendly people.

'I hated America.'

'Really? Why?'

'It frightened me. All those riots and muggings and armed policemen; you can't walk down the streets in New York. It's a violent place. Nobody is safe there.'

Paul raised an eyebrow. 'It's my guess your father would rather be in Philadelphia, as W. C. Fields put it.' But it sounded as if he were moralising, or selling the idea of foreign travel. 'Did you make your fortune these last ten years?' he asked wearily.

'No. The Carnegies and the Fords and the Kennedys got there ahead of me. I'm broke, Mr Temple. Another reason why I had half decided to stay in England. It's an easier place to be poor in. My father was trying to find me a job before he was—' He hesitated superstitiously. 'Before he was strangled.'

'You knew that?' Paul asked. He took another crumpet from Gladys Ashwood's freshly toasted batch and smiled his thanks at her.

'That he died of a broken neck? Yes, the inspector told me yesterday.'

'Of course, he would have done. You are the next of kin. He only told me this afternoon. But I'd like to know what your reaction was. I thought it was very interesting.'

'What's interesting about it?' Ronnie demanded. 'My father is dead. Does it matter, except to my father, whether he was strangled or drowned? This isn't a bloody cross-word puzzle!'

Before Paul could make soothing noises the young man had turned away in distress and Tracy Leonard was being all maternal. He wasn't in tears, but he was tense and strug-gling for self-control. The sound of weeping was coming from Gladys Ashwood.

'This is hardly fair, Mr Temple,' Tracy Leonard said coldly. 'Ronnie was only just on the point of making things up with his father when Mr Kelby died. That leaves an awful lot of free-floating guilt to be carefully handled. There's no real need to play on his feelings of responsibility. And look what you've done to poor Gladys!'

Gladys was stumbling towards the door mumbling: 'It isn't so, it isn't true.' Her crying could be heard all the way down the passage and into the kitchen.

'It's all right,' said Ronnie. 'I suppose he has to break through the facade if he's going to find the killer. And it is interesting, he's perfectly right. Why did Gladys react like that?'

Tracy shrugged as she went to find out.

'You'll need to be clever,' Ronnie added, 'to penetrate Tracy Leonard's facade. I've been trying to get through for nearly a month.'

Paul felt slightly immoral, like a big game hunter, as he followed to do just that. He found Tracy Leonard in the passage outside the kitchen. 'Is Gladys all right?' he asked her.

Tracy nodded.

'The trouble with murder investigations is that all the humdrum secrets we usually live with are singled out for examination. Even the nicest man, by the time his idiosyncrasies have been isolated, can seem to be an alcoholic or an egomaniac, a womaniser or a miser. I'd like you to know how much I admired Alfred Kelby.'

Her large brown eyes were sad as she smiled. 'I didn't admire him, Mr Temple. I was in love with him, as you obviously know, but I despised him. There are no humdrum secrets between a man and his secretary.'

'Was he in love with you?'

'No.'

She led the way through to her quarters in the east wing of the house. It was a single, open-plan room with everything that a large flat would have contained in its split levels and partition cupboards. It had been designed for Tracy Leonard. Paul stood in the doorway for several moments and admired it as a piece of design.

Tracy suddenly fitted in, the tall slender body in flowing black, her lines evoked in movement against the pine walls. It was inevitable suddenly to see the bed on its raised platform, with dressing table and wardrobe, as a shrine facing east in the girl's sanctuary. The total effect was surprisingly feminine and warm.

'I think he loved me once, during the summer I first came here. It was the weather for romance. But then he lost interest, he found someone else. I became just another figure from his past, and a man of that age has a lot of past. I meant almost nothing to Alfred these last four years.'

Paul was staring at a charcoal figure drawing which had been framed and hung on the wall beside a desk. It was Tracy, lying across a divan in sleep. 'He must have been mad,' Paul murmured.

She grinned. 'Thanks.' The wide mouth was open and amused.

'Why did you stay here?'

'I like my flat, and I enjoyed my work. I had the excuse not to face the real problems of being a historian while I was here. Now I shall have to do original work, and I may find I have no originality. That's a discovery I preferred to put off as long as possible.'

Paul sat in a chair that looked like a Le Corbusier copy in tubular steel. 'I would have thought that working with Kelby was good for the originality.' It was a pretty solid chair, better for looking at than sitting in.

'Alfred was fundamentally frivolous, Mr Temple. He had a brilliant mind and he liked to show off with it. He spent too much time appearing on television. Perhaps he was too intelligent to take history seriously. The only thing that history proves is that men are superficial and that turning points are fortuitous, the men in power are not the men in control. So Alfred began to see himself as a natural genius, far more clever than Hitler or Napoleon or Cromwell or Henry VII.

The irony is that he probably was more clever than they, but he proved it by earning money, cracking jokes and sleeping with attractive young girls. He didn't know what else to do. Any other form of power would have seemed to him unsophisticated.'

He was also too kind for other forms of power, Paul thought. He wondered about the reason for her love, why she had needed a man old enough to be her father. Kelby had been gentle in a world of ebullient students, and Tracy for all her physical perfection had been an unworldly girl.

Paul sighed. He was romanticising about her. For all he knew she was a savage and wild animal motivated by her sexual drives. But it didn't matter. He was content to relax for a few minutes in her company.

Tracy went abstractedly up the brief flight of steps and sat down on the bed. She looked down at Paul.

'Who was the girl,' Paul asked, 'at the funeral today?'

'That was Jennie Mortimer. She's younger than I am, which counts with a man like Alfred.'

'Jennie Mortimer?'

'That's right, Ted Mortimer's daughter. She's a nymphet who learned how to make men dance at a very early age.' Tracy laughed maliciously. 'Do you know, she's at a teachers' training college? Alfred had to give her special coaching to get her through her A levels. Her brain isn't where she scores.'

As she spoke with such brutal cynicism a tear ran down her cheek. Paul found the sight quite strangely desolating.

Chapter 9

THE Crown was one of those pubs that had been licensed in the thirteenth century for the accommodation of pilgrims, and it hadn't changed much. The low beams were the kind you bang your head on after ten o'clock and the 'parlour' was built to resemble a parlour; there was no recognisable bar and the customers had to sit round facing each other and talk. Paul went into the public bar.

He ordered a whisky. 'You're quiet here this evening,' he said to the barman.

'We don't fill up till after eight o'clock,' said the barman.

It was a few minutes past seven. 'I suppose all the farmers stay indoors and listen to The Archers?'

The barman was baffled. He was a stout, benevolent man in his late fifties. He tried to be friendly. 'You'll be down from London, I suppose. For the funeral this afternoon.'

'That's right. Poor old Kelby. I suppose he was well known in the village?'

'Ar.' He polished a few glasses while he considered. 'Mr Kelby did a lot for Melford Cross. On the education. And of course he were famous – he used to come in here with people we see on the television.' The barman turned out to be talkative. 'Not that he were stuck up. He came in here sometimes with old Leo Ashwood and had a pint. Mr Kelby was well liked.'

Paul bought the man a drink and gradually turned the conversation to public opinion in the village. Do local people think they know how it happened? Local gossip can be a lot better informed than the police.

'You mean, who do they think drowned him in the rain butt?' the landlord asked incredulously. 'Well, everybody knows who done it, don't they?'

'The police haven't the faintest idea.'

'Ar, yes, well, they're CID from London, aren't they? What would they know about Melford Cross? But the people here know who did it. You ask Inspector Hobden.' He nodded darkly. 'We knowed as soon as Mr Kelby went missing.'

'Inspector Hobden couldn't even tell me the name of Kelby's girlfriend.'

The barman smiled cryptically and said that Hobden had to live with the people of Melford Cross.

'How do they know who done it?' Paul asked.

'A man – a farmer who don't like his animals, Mr Temple, he's a wrong 'un. He'd be capable of killing a man, especially if he had a motive, like money. And that's all Ted Mortimer cares about: money!'

'And his daughter?' Paul asked.

The barman grinned.

Paul bought another whisky and returned to the end of the bar. It was half past seven. Half a dozen local youths had come into the bar and were settling down for a social evening. Paul noted with surprise that the courting couples retained an eighteenth-century mode of behaviour. They arrived in pairs, but then the girls all sat together with their drinks and gossiped about the boys, while the boys all stood together at the bar with their pints and talked cars. Courtship would still be a protracted business in Melford.

Surely, he thought, Ted Mortimer couldn't have murdered Kelby for money, because he would still owe the two thousand pounds to Kelby's estate. If it were Mortimer it would need to be for a different motive. Paul wondered how Kelby came to lend the man two thousand pounds. Something to do with the girl? It was a lot of money for a neighbourly gesture.

His reverie was dispelled by the sight of Leo Ashwood. The chauffeur–handyman came into the bar and ordered a double rum. The barman treated him as a regular, but he was not over-familiar. Leo was obviously well known as a strong silent type. He stood and drank his rum with grim introspection. He hadn't noticed Paul in the corner.

'Hello,' said Paul. 'How's Mrs Ashwood now?'

Leo stared at him for a moment without answering, then he managed to speak. 'She's in bed, sir. Took one of Miss Leonard's sleeping pills and went to bed early. She takes things hard, does Gladys.'

'She was obviously attached to Mr Kelby.'

'He was a good employer.' Leo knocked back the rest of his drink and banged his glass on the counter. 'I must be off. Good night, Mr Temple.'

But he paused by the door and looked back. 'By the way, Mr Temple, you do know that Mr Kelby went across to Galloway Farm on Monday evening, don't you? He was seen there, whatever Ted Mortimer may say.' Then he left.

Detective Inspector Vosper arrived at eight o'clock. He bought half a pint of bitter and took Paul through into the parlour. 'I like to relax when I'm off duty,' he said. 'I don't like people staring at me as if I were a policeman when I'm

drinking.' He raised the half-pint glass. 'Cheers, Temple.'
The three regulars in front of the fire continued to discuss
the *Morecambe and Wise Show* on television and laughed
loudly from time to time. 'Who's the man with the short fat
hairy legs?' one of them called, much to Paul's alarm. But
they took no notice of Paul or the inspector.

'Leo comes in here every night,' said Charlie Vosper confi-
dentially. 'He's been hitting the bottle since his boss was
murdered. Poor devil. Quite convinced that Ted Mortimer
is the murderer.'

'He told me Kelby was seen on Galloway Farm last
Monday evening.'

'The village is seething with rumour.' Charlie puffed at his
pipe and grinned. The off-duty policeman relaxing. 'But all
the rumours seem to emanate from Leo. I can't build a case
on Leo's vendetta against a neighbouring farmer.'

'There's one thing that troubles me,' said Paul. He waited
while Charlie struck some more matches for his pipe, and
then asked why Kelby had been so generous with his money.
'Two thousand pounds is a significant sum even for Kelby.'

'He did it for Leo.'

Paul raised an eyebrow in surprise. 'Not for Jennie?'

'No, I don't think so. Leo and Kelby were very close, and
Leo got himself into serious trouble when Jennie was fourteen.
He had an affair with her. That could have meant prison for
Leo.' Charlie Vosper chuckled at a private joke. 'Jennie used
to visit Melford House after school, and apparently Kelby
gave her some private coaching for her A levels. It looked
rather bad for Kelby as well, actually. Ted Mortimer thought
they were *both* having it off with the girl. But Kelby wasn't,
not at that stage.'

'I see.'

Paul went to the bar and fetched another round of drinks. He could understand why Tracy Leonard had been so upset. It must have been a nasty scene. And the fact that eventually Kelby had lent the man two thousand pounds would only have confirmed his guilt in Tracy's eyes.

'That makes Leo rather a swine,' Paul began when he returned to the chair in the corner.

'I'm not sitting here having a friendly off-duty drink with you for your benefit, Temple,' the inspector interrupted. 'You were going to tell me about the diary. Why have I been warned off?'

They stayed in the smoke-filled parlour for another hour. Paul told him nearly all he knew about the missing diary, although he became rather vague about his visit to Harry in Whitehall.

'You mean government security is involved?' Charlie demanded, 'or that some previous politician's reputation is at stake?'

'No,' said Paul. 'I expect the assistant commissioner still feels that the Delamore murder is his own case.'

By the time Charlie Vosper had cursed the lost opportunity of imprisoning Grover and had told Paul exactly what he thought of the hon. sons of lords who lent their names to shady enterprises he had reduced the atmosphere with his pipe to something like a shunting yard.

But he wasn't happy. 'It's coincidental,' he muttered. 'If they had the diary they didn't need to kill Kelby. Even little Willie Price-Pemberton wouldn't mind now, twenty years later, because he's fallen into obscurity. I always said the diary was irrelevant!'

'I've always agreed with you,' Paul said happily.

Charlie Vosper was angry. 'I know! So what the hell? Why is Sir Philip Tranmere dead?' He hurled a match into the fire. 'I've a good mind to arrest Ted Mortimer and close the bloody case!' He lapsed into gloomy silence.

A telephone was ringing somewhere in the pub, and a few minutes later the barman came in search of Inspector Vosper. He was suitably apologetic, but there had been an incident up at Galloway Farm. Would the inspector go there immediately? To Paul's amazement Charlie said no, they had both been drinking. 'Tell the local force to send a car!'

They reached Galloway Farm at a quarter to ten. There were three police cars in the dirt road to the house with searchlights beamed on the building. From the distance it looked like a southern mansion on party night, with elegant guests milling about in the grounds. Which only emphasised the drab contrast, the neglected air of the house when they reached it, when the guests were visibly policemen.

The policeman on the door reported all quiet. Leo was sitting in the porch with his head between his knees. He didn't look up as they went past him into the kitchen. There Ted Mortimer was having his cuts and bruises tended by his daughter.

'Who called the police?' Inspector Vosper asked.

'I did,' said the girl. 'My father was being beaten up rather severely. I tried throwing water over them, but that didn't help. Leo was drunk.'

There was a young man in plain clothes lurking by the door. Paul didn't need to ask who he was. An earnest young man in a raincoat, wearing spectacles. He said he was waiting for his photographer to arrive.

'Wait for him outside,' said Charlie Vosper. 'When I want the local press I usually send for them.'

The young man winked disconcertingly at Paul and went into the passage.

'He knows what happened already,' said Jennie. 'He must have friends at the local police station. He promised to put my photograph in the paper this week.'

'I told you to keep out of this,' Ted Mortimer said sullenly. 'You don't know what it's like here any more. Ouch!'

She reminded Paul irresistibly of a female second at a wrestling match as she pushed Ted Mortimer's head under the cold water tap. She ignored his cries of pain and set about rubbing ointment into his wounds.

'I know how strong Leo is,' she said with a fierce glare at the police. 'He used to beat me when I was young.' It looked improbable. The girl's soft curves were effectively disguised by the black leather tunic she was wearing. The boots would terrify most professional wrestlers.

'Leo looks quite docile out there at the moment,' Paul murmured.

'He's been out here every night. Banging on the doors and shouting in the road. My father has been living in terror these last few nights. Leo stands out there in the dark and bawls abuse until he passes out. I suppose he wakes up a few hours later and goes home. He hasn't been there when my father gets up at first light.'

'What does he shout about?' Paul asked.

'He accuses my father of killing Alfred Kelby.'

'That's enough, Jennie. It's none of their business. Ouch!' He clutched at his swollen cheek. 'I can fight my own battles.'

'So why haven't you opened the door to Mr Ashwood before?' the inspector asked tactlessly.

'It was common sense not to.'

'Because Leo is a great deal stronger and ten years younger than my father. He's a barroom brawler. Look at these bruises—'

'Ow!' Mortimer grunted. 'Tonight Jennie was here. She opened the door.'

'Nobody terrorises me,' she said with a flick of her blonde hair.

She suddenly picked up a heavy saucepan and hurled it past Paul Temple's right shoulder. Paul ducked, but from the grunt behind him he realised it had been aimed at somebody else. Leo Ashwood had come gingerly into the kitchen with two more policemen.

'I want to prefer charges for assault,' Leo was saying.

'Not in this bloody house you don't!' Jennie shouted.

She flew across the kitchen and attacked Leo with a large oven casserole. The policemen drew back in surprise and watched as the casserole broke into five pieces. Leo cowered against the dresser, hands over his face, quite unprotected as she hitched up her leather skirt and raised her knee sharply into his groin. Amid the flashing of press camera lights Leo sank to the floor in a similar posture to the one he had adopted in the porch.

'If anybody brings a charge of assault,' she said angrily to Vosper, 'it will be my father, against him.'

The policemen clearly didn't know whether to applaud or arrest her, so they grinned among themselves and shifted their weight from foot to foot.

'That will make quite a picture,' said the local reporter from the doorway, 'I liked it.'

'Well,' she said with a shrug, 'I learned how to handle Leo when I was fourteen.'

Vosper shooed the reporter and his cameraman back into the passage and threatened them with charges of trespass and such crimes as interfering with the course of justice. But they didn't seem very deterred. They obviously knew all the uniformed men.

'I'm sorry about this,' Vosper said to Jennie, 'you've obviously got enough problems with your father in this condition—'

Jennie gave a brisk laugh. 'I've been my father's daughter for twenty years. I'm used to him. He has a knack of always landing on his neck. He makes enemies easily and he loses money with every project he's ever taken up. I don't know how he has survived in this farming business for so long. Perhaps it would have been better if we'd let him go bankrupt.'

Ted Mortimer was looking sheepish at being so discussed in front of five policemen. He muttered something about selling up and getting out.

'Let's go,' said Vosper.

They could have charged Leo with behaviour likely to cause a breach of the peace, with or without Ted Mortimer's consent, but Charlie Vosper was bitterly uninterested. He had Leo driven home by police car.

'I won't be a moment,' said Paul. 'I want to have a private word with Jennie.'

'Why? Do you want to ask her about that letter we found? I've already asked her.' He leaned against the porch and lit his pipe. 'It was written to her. She admitted it when I spoke to her this afternoon. She'd written to him care of the education committee at the town hall.'

'Why the secrecy?' Paul asked.

Jennie's voice spoke in the passage behind them. 'Because his son had come home and Alfred didn't want him to know.' She laughed with a sideways glance at the photographer who was sitting on the stairs. 'I think he was embarrassed because Ronnie is older than I am.'

Paul went back to her. 'When was the quarrel between your father and Kelby?' he asked. 'Was that why you wanted to see him?'

She looked surprised. 'I don't think there was a quarrel. Suddenly Alfred began asking for the money back, that was all. That was why I wrote him the letter asking to see him. He was ruining my father.'

Her eyes on closer inspection turned out to be hazel. 'Why did Kelby suddenly want the money back?' he asked.

She shrugged. 'I don't think he did really. But it wasn't a legally contracted loan and my father hadn't signed anything. Alfred needed something legal because of his will.'

'Let's go,' said Vosper.

The inspector gave vent to another outburst against the local press as he passed them. He told them they would be gaoled for contempt of court if they printed a word about the case. It was all *sub judice*. They nodded cheerfully, and asked him how he spelled his name.

'I'd love to pose for you again,' Jennie was saying to them as Paul followed the inspector from the house. 'But I don't use violence on men just because they ask me to. I have to be angry.'

Charlie Vosper drove away from Galloway Farm with a stream of curses against country girls who stir up country passions. It was all beside the point, he claimed. If she wanted to get herself raped, sooner or later . . .

'What is the point?' asked Paul.

'I want to know how Sir Philip Tranmere fits into all this. And little Willie Price-Pemberton. That's the bloody point!'

Chapter 10

IT was past eleven o'clock and Paul had still not come home from wherever he had gone to. It must have been a long funeral. His absence gave Steve the opportunity to do some of those things which he laughed at when he was home. While he had been in America she had used a face pack on three occasions and it hadn't done her complexion any harm. She had given herself a nasty turn when she glimpsed herself in the mirror, and when she smiled it had looked as if her face was flaking. A rather H film contribution to youthful charm.

Bumping noisily along the bedroom floor on her bottom, and hoisting her hips in the air and bicycling with her legs, were much more fun. Steve fundamentally believed in exercise. She lay on the sheepskin rug panting from the exertion of touching her toes twenty times. That would keep her tummy flat and her spirit uplifted!

She went to bed feeling fit and beautiful. Paul claimed to have read somewhere that making love was the physical equivalent of a seven-mile walk, but that was probably because he seldom walked anywhere. It was a relief sometimes to have him out of the house when she was preparing for bed. Novelists can be around the house too much.

She turned out the bedside lamp. Perhaps there had been a wake after the funeral; sending the dead cheerfully on their journey, and renewing life on earth. Steve knew what she would say if Paul arrived home with whisky on his breath. She didn't like the sound of that Tracy Leonard, with her aura of mystery and total self-possession.

What was the point of keeping an ear to the ground in Melford? Sir Philip Tranmere had never been near the place, and they knew Lady Delamore had the diary in her possession. There were two perfectly obvious alternatives to choose from: go and steal the diary back, or telephone Jeremy for a chat about record sleeves.

Jeremy had suggested she stay the night that Wednesday, but he always suggested staying the night to women, it was part of his image. He thought women expected it of him. Steve smiled to herself as she thought how surprised he would be if somebody accepted. She pushed back the bed clothes and slipped out of bed. She dressed quickly in the dark and went quietly out of the house. She took the Hillman Super Imp and drove to the other side of London.

The square was deserted. An all-night bus was creeping into the distance. Steve glanced up at the towering silhouette of the house looming against the night, then she hurried down to the basement flat. She assumed these to be the butler's quarters. They seemed to have direct access to the rest of the house.

Steve slipped a sliver of perspex against the catch and pushed open the door. There were no audible alarms.

She ought not to have been there, of course. Paul still believed somewhere in his mediaeval soul that she was the little woman to be protected, left at home in the warm while he ventured out and faced the world. But she was a stubborn creature. She thought that she had shared so many cases with him and shared so many risks that she was a fully paid up partner in the firm.

Besides, she wanted to read that diary.

She was wearing a black cat suit, big black woolly jumper and soft leather boots, which were more appropriate to a spot of burglary than the beads and bangles which she regarded as the only possible accessories. She jangled as she walked.

The basement door opened directly into the butler's kitchen. Steve picked her way through the clutter of waste bucket and vegetable rack and miscellaneous cans to the sliding door into a narrow corridor. It smelled damp, she was thinking as she kicked over some empty beer bottles.

She waited for three minutes, but the butler did not appear. The gentle snores from a room along the corridor on the right continued evenly. So Steve took a pencil torch from her belt and lit the way to the bottom of the stairs.

'Keep to the wall,' she murmured to herself, the first law of burglary, 'because all stairs creak.'

The stairs creaked. She ran up three at a time against the wall and then stopped to listen again. There was no movement from the butler's bedroom.

She emerged from what looked like a broom cupboard into the main hall. The front door was bristling with wires that could only lead to burglar alarms. Steve shone the torch briefly against each door and up the stairs.

The door into Lady Delamore's drawing room was at the end of the hall. The floors were thick with carpets, which helped her to move soundlessly and fast to the door. It was the room where Steve had been received on Thursday so she knew the geography without falling over armchairs.

A faint moonlight helped as Steve set about searching the room. She felt behind all the cushions, moved the books in

91

the bookcase and looked in a cupboard in the corner. The escritoire by the window was locked, so Steve prepared to work on it with a hair grip.

A chauffeur-driven car drew up in the street outside. Steve watched as two men got out of the car and went up to the door of Delamore House. They knocked with the heavy authority of the police. And almost at once there were footsteps on the stairs, the front door was opened and there were voices in the hall.

Steve looked about her in alarm, and was struggling to hide in the window when the drawing room lights were turned on.

Chapter 11

IT was nearly midnight. The Thames near Marlow threaded into a black nothing of fields and towpaths, with barely a light from the houseboats moored alongside to show them the way. The water lapped noisily against the hulks, and occasionally a fish surfaced, splashed, and left a strange silence behind, to be broken eventually by the rustle of a vole or water rat in the bank.

'What a strange place to choose to live,' Charlie Vosper whispered loudly.

Paul guided him back onto the path. 'It has its charm, inspector. Away from the hurly burly of London.'

'It's so damned noisy! Listen to that owl.'

It was noisy. The houseboats creaked a lot, and there was a breeze crackling through the trees.

'I like the hurly burly of London,' said Charlie Vosper.

The river formed a natural basin in the bow downstream from the weir, and the basin was lined with houseboats. A colony inhabited by weekend people and actors and retired sea captains. About thirty-five people conspiring to keep out the real world, to preserve a life invented by Kenneth Grahame with an added dash of the King's Road, Chelsea.

An exactly suitable place for Willie Price-Pemberton to pass his declining years. He could sit on the poop deck on Sunday mornings and watch the leggy girls in sailor hats empty the sluices and fetch the milk.

Willie Price-Pemberton claimed that you saw all of life from the poop deck of the *Gay Deceiver*, or at least all of it that he wanted to see; which was very little. A few female bottoms, a hairy male torso once in a while, the sight of a boat rocking on Sunday afternoons in a still river, and his cat Madge. Willie was an observer now, not a doer. A cat lover.

'It's never dark like this in London,' Charlie Vosper whispered.

'What do you want to see?'

'Bloody bogeymen, Temple, that's what. I keep thinking we're being followed.'

Paul chuckled. Then he stopped chuckling and laid a hand on Vosper's arm. 'Stay still,' he whispered. 'We're being followed.' The snapping of dry twigs and as he came closer the distinct outline of a man confirmed the fact.

'Let's go back,' urged Charlie. 'I've been warned off—'

'You're with me,' said Paul, 'remember? I haven't been warned off.'

'You're just not supposed to be here.'

'That's right.'

A quick flash of Paul's pencil torch confirmed that they had reached the *Gay Deceiver*. The gangplank was moving gently beside them as the breeze took the boat downstream and the tension of its moorings pulled it back, a gentle swaying motion that should be lulling Willie into a deeper, fuller sleep.

While they remained by the gangplank indecisively wondering whether to go back or surreptitiously nip aboard, the footsteps caught up with them and a strong torch was shone in their faces.

Paul took out a cigarette and asked the man for a light.

'Don't you dare make a fight for it, Temple,' said the voice from the darkness.

'Harry! I should have guessed it was you.'

'And I guessed that this was where you would be coming. Vosper, what the hell are you doing here?'

'Just keeping an eye on Mr Temple, sir.'

'I shall forget I ever saw you here. Now sod off back to London.'

They were interrupted by a voice from the direction of the river. 'I say there, are you going to be talking all night? Move along, there's someone trying to get some sleep here!'

'You aren't going to sleep yet, Price-Pemberton. Unbatten the hatches and let us aboard.' Harry strode up the gangplank. He pulled back the tarpaulin over the steering cabin and jumped down. Paul followed. The last they saw of Charlie Vosper that night was the flare of a match as he lit his pipe. A few moments later Charlie went.

'Go away,' cried Price-Pemberton. 'It's gone twelve o'clock!'

Harry sat at the disused wheel of the boat, took out his hip flask and fortified himself against the damp air. He offered the flask to Paul, who shook his head. 'All right,' said Harry, 'you persuade the silly arse to open up.'

Paul introduced themselves through a tiny open port-hole. He explained that they'd come to talk because Sir Philip Tranmere had committed suicide. They thought Willie might be in trouble as well, so they'd come to help. Nothing happened inside the boat. Paul explained that the trouble was all because of Margaret Spender's diary.

'You'd better come in,' said Price-Pemberton. He unbolted the hatch and let them through. 'Are you going to arrest me?' he asked.

'No,' said Harry. 'You remember me. I'm the friendly policeman who investigated Lord Delamore's death in 1947.'

Price-Pemberton was a small, bald and flabby man with a white face and quick nervous movements. His eyes were surprisingly keen in the inert face. He was wrapped in a voluminous dressing gown, so that when he sat on his bunk he looked like a small Buddha. From the way the houseboat was decorated it was obvious that little Willie pampered himself. Expensive drapes on the walls, rare books and old masters, elegant furniture; what there was in the small bedsitting boat was the very best.

'I suppose you bullied poor Rover into committing suicide.'

'Rubbish,' Harry said cheerfully.

Paul watched suspiciously as Harry settled his bulky frame into a Sheraton chair. He wasn't at all sure what Harry was doing here. But when Harry sat quietly and unaggressively back and let someone else do the explaining it usually meant trouble. Harry always meant trouble.

'Sir Philip committed suicide because his exploits during August 1947 were recorded in Margaret Spender's diary.

'And the diary is about to be published. I suppose he couldn't bear the idea of living through all that again.'

Willie Price-Pemberton blinked a few times, but he said nothing. A seal point Siamese cat jumped on to Willie's lap and he stroked it absentmindedly.

'The diary names you as the murderer of Lord Delamore.'

'It was all a long time ago,' said Willie.

'Were you Lady Delamore's lover?'

'Of course not. I was a junior diplomat, and her husband was very high up in the service—'

'You made love to her on three recorded occasions.'

A few beads of sweat appeared on Willie's bald dome. 'That's not at all the same thing,' he said pedantically to the cat. 'Anyway, she made love to me. I didn't take the initiative.'

'I know,' said Harry. 'Lady Delamore claimed you were sexually inadequate; that was what she told all your friends. There's a very amusing description in the diary of you taking a bath at the shooting lodge—'

'Madge used to do it deliberately. She humiliated men to be revenged on her husband. It's all in Freud, you know, it's a perfectly standard behaviour pattern. She took advantage of her husband's rank to humiliate me.'

Harry was laughing unsympathetically. 'The diary says you were infatuated with her.'

'I was much younger at the time. I thought she was a nymphomaniac and I let her fascinate me. But she wasn't, she only claimed to be a nymphomaniac to make herself more interesting. She was frigid.'

'I don't need convincing,' Harry said indifferently.

'I'm like everybody else, I just enjoy a good joke. Those neighbours of yours will fall into the river with laughing when they read about you. Little Willie, that's what they'll call you again.'

Willie's hands were trembling as he stroked the cat, and as if it sensed that something was wrong the cat stopped its noisy purring. 'Would you like a drink?' Willie asked flatly. 'I think I need one.'

'I thought you were never going to offer.' Harry went instinctively to the galley cupboard where the whisky and soda were kept. He returned with the three glasses and officiated himself. He kept the bottle by him.

'That was the most hellish summer I've ever spent,' said Willie. 'The world was a better place, marginally, without

Lord Delamore. He deliberately made trouble between Rover Tranmere and me. He thought it amusing.'

Willie Price-Pemberton stared at his whisky and became almost tranquil as he remembered the events.

'Rover Tranmere was Madge's lover, not me.'

'What happened?' Harry asked.

'He challenged me to a duel.'

'Isn't that a little out of date?' asked Harry.

'Oh yes, totally. I'd never handled a pistol in my life. But Madge Delamore thought it would be amusing, so I had to meet Rover at dawn. I didn't really know how to avoid the encounter. They were so excited by their game, and they had this pair of antique duelling pistols.'

Paul was taken aback. 'Did you know about this?' he asked Harry.

'Yes, it's in the diary. But I didn't know at the time.'

'How do you know what's in the diary?'

'Ssh,' he said. 'Carry on, Willie.'

'Well, Rover and I fought our duel in a clearing in the woods, the clearing where the third Lord Delamore had been killed in 1792. It was rather a nice morning, actually, with the sun melting through the early morning mists. Lord Delamore was the only other person present, he was the referee or master of ceremonies, whatever it's called. He brought us together and put us back to back. I remember feeling light-headed, because I thought I was bound to be killed. Rover Tranmere was a very famous soldier. But in fact we walked our fifteen paces, turned and fired at each other, and Lord Delamore dropped to the ground with a bullet in his head.'

Little Willie giggled to himself. 'Rover and I both ran like mad back to the shooting lodge. I wouldn't know which of us shot him. But it was an accident.'

'Do you realise what will happen when this story is published?' Harry asked.

'Yes,' said Willie.

'You'll be overwhelmed by reporters and we'll probably see you on the Frost Programme.'

'I'll have another drink,' said Willie. 'While there's still some left.'

Paul was still troubled by the reason behind Harry's visit; he knew that any good defence lawyer would get little Willie acquitted of any charges. And even Harry knew that because he wasn't about to make an arrest. They were leaving.

'Is that all?' asked Willie.

'That's all. I only came to see how you were. Just checking to see whether you were fit and healthy. Come on, Temple, let's get out before the publicity machine descends on him.' He shook hands with little Willie. 'It's been a pleasure to meet a man like you, Mr Price-Pemberton, there isn't much old-fashioned sense of honour left. And I must admit I enjoy a good laugh.'

Paul followed him up onto the deck. They left Willie Price-Pemberton downstairs, ashen on his bunk, stroking the Siamese cat. He didn't say goodbye.

They felt their way to the bank in the dark and went slowly off along the towpath. Paul didn't speak for several minutes.

'Is that what you did to Sir Philip Tranmere?' he eventually asked Harry.

'That's right. Slightly different dialogue, but the end result was the same.' They walked on in silence until Harry felt that some justification was required of him.

'Listen, I don't ask those silly arses to commit suicide. What I ask is that they keep quiet, go into hiding, hire a good lawyer, anything. But I'm not having them go on television making me look a fool or giving extra impetus to a scandal.'

'You didn't do that to Kelby, did you?'

'Of course not. Kelby wasn't involved in Delamore's death.'

They reached the ministry car and climbed inside. The driver moved off at once, and Harry barked: 'Delamore House' at him before sinking back into his seat.

Well, at least they hadn't killed him themselves. He felt rather like crying, but instead he lifted Madge up to his cheek and brushed his face against the fur. Poor Madge: she hadn't done anything to deserve this. He wondered what would happen to her. Perhaps they'd take her to some hospital and experiment on her. He couldn't bear the thought of that.

He poured the remaining whisky into a tumbler and tried to compose himself. He lit a cigarette. There was no reason why he shouldn't chain smoke now. Finish the whole packet. No need to be afraid of cancer. No need to fear any of the usual things, like the neighbours laughing at him or falling into the river and drowning. Although drowning was supposed to be a peaceful death. It was what his father used to do to the kittens.

He sipped at the whisky. The warm excitement flowed through his blood. For the first time in years he felt contented, in control of his own life. He didn't even feel resentment against the grey block of a man who had drunk most of the whisky. Nor against the young man who'd sat in the corner so aloofly.

Sixty years was enough anyway. He had learned all there was to know about himself, done the things he'd been meant to do and given up early. The past ten years on the boat had been pleasant, but repetitive, even boring really. He was grateful for the sudden intrusion of drama. People would find him interesting, try to remember who he had been, and they would call him enigmatic. He didn't feel like crying. He felt sad, that was all, nostalgic for someone he had never been. Sad at the failure of it all.

'Come along, Madge,' he murmured. 'Your country calls you.'

He finished the whisky, lit another cigarette, and turned out all the lights. He closed the hatches and tied down the tarpaulins as he left the boat. There was no point, but it was tidy. He wondered absurdly whether to cancel the milk. There was a tear running down his left cheek, he discovered as he smiled. But it was sadness, he told himself, not fear.

'I can't leave you behind,' he whispered to Madge. 'They'd use your fur for those silly fur coats. It isn't a fit world for a sensitive cat.'

Madge miaowed loudly in reply. Cats are human too.

He set off upstream along the towpath. He was glad it was so dark. It meant that nobody would see him crying. The couple in the next boat were quarrelling again. Normally he enjoyed listening to their rows. The young man always ended by beating her, and next morning she would appear on deck with some interesting bruises. But tonight he felt that their quarrels were such a waste of life. The girl was young and red haired and full bosomed. She was yelling for help as she always did.

There was a stockbroker in the next boat. He was old, more than sixty-five, grim faced and ruthless. One of these evenings he would die of a heart attack, his false teeth buried in that dull secretary's buttocks again. It was an inevitable comedy. People spend so much of their time and ingenuity in hard pursuit of love, even stockbrokers, he reflected. Even Mrs Dalgleish, who lived alone in the boat beside the stockbroker. She was the only atheist he knew who bought altar candles and called out Christ in the night. Even the young married couple along the moorings hadn't settled down to watching television; they swopped partners at weekends with trendy friends from the London suburbs. He wondered whether to feel sad for them all. The big boat belonged to Captain Blair, who drank a bottle of rum every day and kept falling off the gangplank. Captain Blair missed the life of adventure he'd been used to at Gosport. A small man with ginger whiskers and red eyeballs.

All of life, he murmured to himself as he looked back at the thirty-five boats concealed in the night. There wasn't really anything more, except the diplomatic corps and shooting holidays and the world behind the television screen. Maybe there had been, in the early years of the century, but not since 1947.

Madge was struggling to get away. It was the noise of the weir that frightened her. But the noise was partly why they had come to this spot: it would drown the shouts if his nerve at the last moment failed him. He knelt on the ground by the iron causeway across the weir and tied a piece of cord to Madge's collar. He tied a brick to the other end of the cord. It was a heavy brick from the derelict wall of the old lock, already soaked with water.

'It's all for the best,' he said to the cat. 'You'll be safer.'

He carried her and the brick to the centre of the iron causeway. She was beginning to panic; the deep pool of water beneath them was black and invisible. The falling water roaring over the weir reflected white shimmers and stars from somewhere. The cat suddenly wriggled free, scratching his hands in a final determined leap. She fell nine feet into the water, but he didn't hear the splash.

That was what happened, he thought self-pityingly, to people who depended on him. He tossed the last cigarette away and wished he had drunk some more whisky. He was a coward. He wiped the tears away, and then realised it was unnecessary. No point in taking off his clothes either. He put up his hand to hold his nose and jumped.

The cries for help were lost in the deafening roar of the weir, and by the time his body drifted away from the swirling water below the falls he was dead.

The little grey-haired old lady was as daunting as Steve had described her. She kissed Harry on the cheek, which showed nerve, and as she offered Paul a frail hand to shake she told him he was too good looking. 'I prefer my men a little more rugged,' she said. 'You look more suitable for the drawing room. Why don't you sit down?'

Paul sat down.

'I've sent poor Simpson to bed,' she explained. 'Young people need their sleep, I seem to remember. And when Simpson is kept out of his bed after one o'clock he smashes plates and yawns as he opens the door. Harry, darling, will you pour Mr Temple whatever he drinks and help yourself to the whisky?'

Harry poured the whiskies.

'I had the pleasure of meeting your wife, Mr Temple, yesterday or last month. Such a charming girl, and very persistent. I hope she discovered whatever she wanted to know from me?'

'Yes, she did,' said Paul. 'She confirmed that you had Margaret Spender's diary.'

She laughed. 'My son gave it to me. He thought I'd be hurt by what poor Margaret had written of Dickie and myself. He's a dutiful boy, but conventional in a rather tiresome way. I sometimes wish I'd never gone through with all that

103

messy business of childbirth. I might have kept my youth now. I found the diary highly amusing. And it brought back so many fond memories. Didn't you think, Harry?'

'I feel happier now that the gossip can't be authenticated.'

'I'd forgotten how amusing my late husband was. He used to make love in his socks and vest, which apparently Margaret Spender hated. That was something I had forgotten.'

'Come on, Madge,' said Harry, 'let's get it over with.'

She went to a delicate little escritoire in the corner of the room and took out a small packet. 'Poor little Willie,' she sighed, 'and poor Rover. They were such fun that summer.' She smiled sadly at Paul and gave him the packet. 'This is for you.' It contained a diary, octavo sized and bound in calf.

'Is this it?' Paul asked in surprise.

There was a jangling sound from the direction of the window. It was like a gentle breeze through a scarecrow. Lady Delamore sniffed and looked about suspiciously.

'That's it,' said Harry. 'You can give it to your friend Scott Reed. Tell him he can go ahead and publish it now.'

Paul was flicking through the green ink pages when Lady Delamore asked him whether he used Adagio perfume. He sighed and assured her he never used scent and bathed daily. No hair oil and he shaved with broken beer bottles.

'Then we must have a burglar.'

She prodded savagely into the curtains behind her.

'Ouch!'

Lady Delamore pulled the sash which drew the curtains back in a dramatic clatter of steel rollers. Paul and Harry rose simultaneously to their feet prepared for battle. But then they relaxed. Huddled in a corner was a slim black burglar which uncoiled bashfully into Steve Temple. She blinked at them and tried to grin.

'Why, Mrs Temple, how unexpected. You must have arrived a few minutes before your husband. I thought I heard beads jangling in the hall. I suppose you came up through the basement.'

She nodded.

'I do hope you didn't wake up Simpson as you passed his quarters,' Lady Delamore said severely. 'He gets very frightened of burglars and is quite liable to give in his notice tomorrow.'

'No,' Steve murmured, 'I was very quiet.' She turned angrily on her husband. 'What are you laughing at, you big ape?'

'There's a piece of your face flaking off.'

Steve was saying something enigmatic about seeing Jeremy instead when Paul interrupted with the formal introductions.

'Harry, you remember my wife, Steve.'

Harry nodded. 'I could never forget those flashing green eyes.'

They led Steve from the house complaining bitterly about orgies and improbably long funeral ceremonies. She must, Paul concluded, have been at the slimming pills again.

Chapter 12

'HARRY said publish and be damned,' Paul repeated wearily.
'A perfectly harmless little man committed suicide last night,
so the diary can do nobody any harm.'

Paul had been trying to work. It had been a spare hour
to use constructively before Scott Reed arrived to collect
the diary. Paul had been sitting at the massive desk with
his hands over his ears, staring at the typewriter. It was the
kind of desk which Dickens had worked at, words tumbling
off his pen, characters like Quilp and Sykes and Magwitch
seething through his imagination. Paul's mind was a total
vacuum. Even with his hands over his ears the only thing he
was aware of was the stereophonic din of guitars and drums,
a piercing blues voice lamenting the fate of a hell's angel.

'Couldn't we turn that down a little?' he asked mildly.

She didn't answer. She hadn't heard. She was sitting with
her sketch pad in the Swedish silence chair. Paul turned off
the record player and returned to his desk.

'Paul! I need that music. My sleeve copy has to be deliv-
ered ready for the printer on Monday. I need to play the
record until it has worked on my unconscious and suggested
its own design.'

'You can't hear it in that chair.' He beat a quick pattern with his fingers on the fibreglass shell. 'It suggests to my very battered conscious mind all hell let loose.'

'Very witty. Darling, you aren't turned on. This is a group that is really underground, what they call a group's group.'

'Why not a cover of the group in an underground tunnel with a tube train thundering up behind them?'

Steve waited patiently for him to finish laughing. 'Jeremy is convinced this will top the LP charts.'

'I never was very impressed by Jeremy's taste. He has such an eye for the obvious.' He stopped and then pointed a finger at Steve. 'Which reminds me, Mrs Temple. What did you mean last night by wishing you'd gone to see Jeremy instead?'

'That's nice,' she murmured. 'So you think I'm obvious, do you?'

'You can be pretty direct.' He laughed. 'Did you hear about Jeremy and that girl who designed book jackets for him? He asked her to stay the night and she stayed. The police were called at three o'clock in the morning to rescue him. He'd fled naked into the street and was cowering in a telephone box.'

'Liar. Why don't you do some work on your book?'

'Maybe I'll make Jeremy the victim, killed in the first chapter. That would teach him a lesson. Slaughtered in a telephone box. People will think he went into the phone box to use his antiperspirant spray. And it was actually a liquid sulphuric acid spray. That's what can happen to people who undress in telephone boxes.'

'As long as you don't make me the villain,' said Steve.

'You'd make a good villain.' Paul laughed, his good humour restored. 'Let's get rid of Scott as quickly as we can.

We should eat out tonight, go to a theatre perhaps. Let's go somewhere luxurious, so that I can remind you what good company I am.'

She poked out her tongue. 'I have a design to finish.'

'Remind me to punch Jeremy on the nose next time I see him.'

Paul put the needle back on the record. He tried to convince himself that the music was relevant to his theme of gratuitous violence. He decided that a novel on the subject would be gratuitous.

'You'd have to compose yourself to die,' Paul murmured, 'whether you're hanged near Hindhead or drowned near Marlow. Little Willie was the type who'd be afraid of pain and he'd hate the cold. I suppose he was brave. And at least his death had intentionality.'

'Yes, dear.' Steve was dabbing the three sample colours on three different tracings of her design. 'Last stage coming up.'

'I suppose Kelby must have been pretty scared as well.'

'Poor Kelby.' Steve put her arms round Paul's neck from behind. 'Do you know who murdered him?'

'Yes, probably. But God knows what we can do about it. The key to the whole case is Grover—'

The front doorbell rang.

'That must be Scott,' Steve said. 'It's all right, darling, I'll let him in.'

Paul unlocked the drawer and took out the diary, experiencing a moment of dread in case it wasn't there. But there it was. A troublesome and unnecessary document.

'Mr Temple?' a woman's voice was asking in the hall downstairs.

'What is it?' Steve asked in bewilderment. 'Are you ill?'

'Tell your husband—'

Paul hurried out to the landing and saw Gladys Ashwood slumped against the door, her arms outstretched, her face clenched in horror. Paul ran down the stairs four at a time.

'What's happened, Gladys?' he called.

She tried to raise her head to look at him. 'He knew,' she gasped. 'About being strangled . . . in the car.' Her eyes closed and she collapsed onto Steve. The dead weight sent Steve reeling back against the stairs and they both fell to the floor in a heap. Gladys Ashwood's body was stretched across Steve's. Paul could see the knife between her shoulder blades.

'Paul!' Steve shouted. 'Paul! Where are you going?'

Paul ran out into the mews. It was almost dark now and the fog had made visibility worse. He could just make out the tail lights of a taxi turning into Chester Square. And there was somebody coming across the street. A man with light footsteps. The stranger in the mews turned out to be Scott Reed.

'Steve, call a doctor,' Paul shouted. 'And after that ring Charlie Vosper.'

'Help me up!' she replied.

Scott Reed was breathless and dishevelled. His clothes were dusty and there was a cut over his forehead. He didn't speak when Paul took his arm and led him upstairs. He stared numbly at Mrs Ashwood's body draped over Steve, but he didn't say anything.

'Careful how you move her, Steve, and don't touch the knife.'

Gladys Ashwood was dead. It took about an hour for the murder squad to go through the same routine as Paul had watched on Thursday. Photographs and fingerprints, preliminary details of time and place, taking away the body. Meanwhile Steve was bathing Scott's forehead and making soothing noises. It was all becoming, Paul reflected, repetitious. He wasn't surprised that Charlie Vosper arrived on the scene in a mood of blustering irritability.

Steve made things worse by asking him after Sir Graham.

'As far as I know he's very fit, Mrs Temple,' snapped Vosper. 'We don't see a great deal of the commissioner, and then not to ask after his health.'

Paul had to turn away while he controlled his grin. He wondered whether Steve had done it deliberately.

'How are you feeling now, Mrs Temple?'

'I've just had a very large drink, inspector. I feel a lot better.'

Vosper leaned over and examined Scott Reed's forehead. The publisher was trying to stand, but he was in obvious pain and he sank back into the chair. Vosper clucked unsympathetically and then consulted a sergeant's notebook.

'Mrs Temple,' he said in puzzlement, 'are you quite sure Mrs Ashwood said: "He knew about being strangled in the car"?'

'Yes.'

'Is that all she said?'

'Well, yes. Then she collapsed with a knife in her back.'

'He knew about being strangled in the car,' the inspector repeated to himself. 'I wonder what she meant by that.'

It seemed to Paul a pretty unanswerable question, so he went to the cocktail cabinet and replenished people's glasses. 'How about you, Charlie, would you like a drink?'

'I'll have a whisky when this sergeant has left the room,' said Vosper. 'I'm on duty. I don't see what was so important about her message that she came all this way to London, or that someone had to kill her to stop her going into detail.'

'If you ask me,' Scott Reed piped surprisingly from his chair in the window, 'she was probably trying to say something about poor old Alfred.'

Vosper swung on him. 'What makes you think that, sir?'

'Well, I mean, wasn't Kelby strangled before he was put in the rain butt?'

'Yes, he was. I know that, sir, and the police doctor, even the coroner now, we all know that. But how do you know it, sir? We simply told the press he'd been found in a rain butt at Galloway Farm.'

Scott was visibly flustered. 'It was in the paper. I read somewhere that Kelby was strangled before he was put in the vat.' He looked helplessly across at Paul. 'Wasn't he strangled?'

'The full story was in the evening papers yesterday, Charlie, every detail.' The sergeant had gone so Paul gave Charlie Vosper his whisky. 'They don't only print what you tell them, I'm afraid.'

Charlie held up his glass in salute and muttered something about Ted Mortimer blabbing to the whole world. 'Some people never learn to keep their mouths shut,' he said to Scott. 'But anyway, let's hear your version of what happened tonight, sir. I've heard Mrs Temple's story.'

Scott was hazy about what had happened. 'I was walking towards the mews when a taxi drove past me. I recognised the occupant; it was Gladys Ashwood. When I arrived at the mews she'd already got out of the taxi. Then I heard the sounds of a scuffle and the next thing I knew someone was running towards me. He was running towards the entrance, and he obviously didn't see me because—'

'How do you know he didn't see you, sir?'

'It was very dark, well, nearly dark but quite foggy. Anyway he ran headlong into me. He would hardly have run into me if he'd seen me, would he, inspector?'

Vosper refused to be drawn. 'Go on, sir.'

'He knocked me over. And as I was falling I made a grab for his legs. Not to attack him really, more an instinctive grab to support myself. And you know what happened? He kicked out and hit me in the face. I was lucky I wasn't blinded.'

'That's reassuring,' said Charlie Vosper. 'Tell me what he looked like.'

'Eh? Well, it was dark, and foggy.'

'Would you recognise him again if you saw him?'

Scott shook his head unhappily. Even that made him wince with pain. 'No. The only thing I can tell you about him was that he—he was about my height and a great deal heavier. Well built, I would say. But I certainly wouldn't recognise him again.'

The inspector had been questioning Scott as if he thought him a murderer. To Paul's relief he quickly changed his manner. He sat beside Scott Reed and sighed. 'Do you think the man was already in the mews? Waiting for Mrs Ashwood when the taxi arrived?'

'Yes, I think he must have been,' said Scott. He was so grateful for the new friendly Vosper that he went into detail. 'It's my bet he was standing in the shadows near the opposite garage.'

'Yes,' Charlie Vosper agreed, 'that seems very likely. Very likely indeed. Thank you, Mr Reed. By the way, one of my men picked up a shoe out there. Quite a nice brogue slip-on shoe.' The inspector produced the shoe with all the panache of a conjuror. 'What do you think of this, Mr Reed?'

'I don't know.' Scott took the shoe and examined it. 'I suppose I might have pulled it off his foot when the brute was kicking me, or when I fell and grabbed him.'

Paul asked to see the shoe. It was a size nine, he found, and handmade. 'Colson's of Bond Street,' he murmured. 'Our friend has very expensive tastes.'

'Colson's?' Scott asked in surprise.

'Yes. Of Bond Street.'

The inspector was staring at Scott. 'What were you going to say, sir?'

'Nothing.' Scott was wriggling again in discomfort.

'You must have been going to say something,' the inspector persisted.

Paul intervened. 'It looks as if Scott buys his shoes from Colson's. They're very nice shoes. Is that what you were going to say, Scott?'

'Yes,' he admitted. 'But I'm not the only one. Lots of my friends buy their shoes from Colson's.'

Paul looked across at Steve and smiled sadly. The jigsaw puzzle was complete in his mind, but there was not a scrap of indictable evidence. Demonstrating the guilt of the murderer would be difficult, and highly dangerous.

'Charlie,' he said, pouring the inspector another drink without asking, 'I want to talk to you.'

The regiment of law and forensic workers were departing. Vosper sat grimly on the sofa next to the publisher.

'Policemen buy their shoes from Freeman Hardy & Willis,' he muttered.

Scott Reed sprang to his feet. 'I really must be going. My wife— forty odd miles to Hambledon.' Before Steve could offer him a bite to eat he fled into the mews clutching his valuable package.

'A very nervous man,' said Charlie Vosper. He looked balefully across the room at Paul and sighed. 'Well, what do you want to talk to me about?'

'Do you know who murdered Kelby?'

'No. I wouldn't be surprised if it were you and that bloody boss of mine. You're a right couple of cowboys.'

'Don't be petulant, Charlie.'

113

'Petulant? Poor little Willie Price-Pemberton is dead!'

Paul nodded. 'I read about it.'

'How can I run an efficient detective squad when my boss regards whole areas of a case as his private business? I told the assistant commissioner this morning, I don't give a damn who murdered Kelby!'

'What did he say?'

'He told me not to be petulant.'

'Quite right, Charlie. You care deeply who killed him, and so do I. As for killing Gladys Ashwood, I feel really vindictive about that. She was a nice old woman and she was trying to help us.'

'I know.' Charlie Vosper finished his drink in silence. 'All right,' he said when he had composed himself. 'I become angry when people from above interfere with my work.' He smiled tentatively. 'Did you see the evening paper tonight? That made me angry as well.'

'What was in the paper?'

Charlie took the folded up evening paper from his raincoat and tossed it across to Paul. There was a photograph of a very photogenic Jennie Mortimer with her skirt up to her thighs kneeing Leo Ashwood in the groin. The Oxfordshire reporter had been given his own byline in the London newspaper: 'Student Teacher Had Secret Tryst with Murdered Historian'. By Jack Armitage. It was a long story and by most standards well written. It described how Jennie Mortimer had had a date to meet Kelby at ten o'clock to discuss her father's debt.

'At ten o'clock last Monday night Alfred Kelby was dead. The police were called to the home of his ex-mistress last night to sort out a brawl which developed between . . .'

114

Paul looked up in horror. 'This story will get Jennie Mortimer murdered.'

'Well,' said Charlie, 'I know it isn't accurate reporting, and I told that bugger Armitage I'd have him for contempt of court, but—'

'Her life is in danger!' Paul threw the newspaper back at him. 'Don't you realise what this says? That at roughly the time Alfred Kelby was murdered he was supposed to be meeting Jennie in the field behind his house! So Jennie would have been at the most two hundred yards away. She could have seen the murder, and she would certainly have seen the murderer pass by on his way to dump the body on Mortimer's farm.'

'Yes, but—'

'But nothing! Don't you know why Gladys Ashwood was killed tonight? Don't interrupt while I'm thinking aloud! She was killed because our murderer is on the run. She was on to him, and now he'll think Jennie is on to him. He's desperate, Charlie, he'll kill again with no compunction whatever.'

Vosper was bewildered. 'Do you think Jennie Mortimer saw it happen?'

'Maybe not, but if our murderer is to cover his tracks he'll have to get rid of her just in case.'

'Blast that fellow Armitage!' Vosper stood up in dismay. 'Look here, Temple. Do you know who this killer is?'

'Of course I do.'

'So, what's the next move?' Charlie Vosper didn't often say things like that. He was a worried man. 'Come on, you tell me for a change. What do we do?'

'We must look after Jennie Mortimer. If we can keep her safe for the next twenty-four hours she might live long enough to be raped and murdered in her own right. But it will take twenty-four hours to solve this case. At the moment we could never prove a thing.' Paul smiled reassuringly at the policeman. 'Don't worry. I'll give you the proof, Charlie. I promise you, I'll give you the proof.'

As Charlie Vosper prepared to leave there was a ring at the doorbell downstairs. 'I'll let them in,' Charlie said as he shook hands with Steve. 'Good night.'

Paul watched him out from the landing. He watched Charlie Vosper open the front door and heard him say: 'What the hell!' Jennie Mortimer was standing on the step with an evening paper in one hand and a weekend case in the other.

Chapter 13

'MY dear Mrs Temple, I've been set up as the next murder victim. Did you expect me to sit pathetically at home and wait for the knife in my back? Look at this newspaper report!'

'Don't you have a big strong boyfriend you could stay with?' Steve asked icily.

Jennie shrugged. 'It was your good-looking husband who did all the talking in front of that reporter. So why can't he protect me until the killer is caught?'

Paul picked up the suitcase and carried it upstairs. 'You're very welcome to stay.' He passed Steve on the landing. 'Isn't she, darling?'

'Of course. Darling.'

'Let me show you to the guest room,' said Paul.

He led her upstairs to the room opposite their bedroom. A murderer would have to climb fifty feet of sheer wall to reach the window, or come up through the inside of the house. Paul watched her bounce on the bed and wondered whether she was truly afraid of death. She grinned at him.

'I'm sorry,' said Paul. 'I ought to have known better than talk to you about that meeting in front of Jack Armitage. It was obvious he would print it.'

'I think you did it deliberately.'

It was difficult to imagine Jennie dead. Her body was so full of life and pleasure. To destroy her, Paul decided, would be evil.

'I'll leave you to settle in.'

Downstairs Steve was clearing up with grim ostentation. She clattered about in the kitchen and then spoke to Paul about the girl's comfort with brittle formality.

'I didn't know she would turn up here,' he said lamely.

'I'm not complaining.'

Paul poured himself a whisky. 'It's all right. I'll soon have this case cleared up.'

'Good.'

'The poor girl is scared.'

'So I see.'

It was a difficult evening. Steve became heavily ironic about the big manly protector, and then Jennie came downstairs to suggest they throw a party. 'It would take our minds off this awful business . . .' No party. But the girl spent the next forty minutes on a series of telephone calls to advise her friends that she was alive and well and living with Paul Temple. Paul Temple opened another bottle of whisky, and Steve went up to wash her hair.

'Your wife's a bit peeved, isn't she?'

Paul turned round and nodded. 'Slightly.' The girl had changed into clothes she could relax in.

'Are you in love with her?'

'Of course.'

'She looks pretty tough. I don't suppose you stood a chance once she had decided to marry you.' Jennie draped herself along the sofa. 'Shall we stay up talking all night? I can tell you the story of my life, for your next novel. Shall

I tell you how I seduced Leo Ashwood? I did it for a dare; I could tell from the way he was always staring at me that he was twisted up with frustration. He used to stand behind me while I was playing—'

'I'd rather hear about Alfred Kelby.'

'I didn't seduce Alfred. He was a sort of father to me. I think he was trying to make up for what Leo had done, poor thing.' She laughed with her mouth open. 'Alfred was really an English gentleman. He accepted responsibility for the actions of his servants. We didn't sleep together till I was nineteen. Tracy Leonard was his mistress.'

'Not for several years past,' said Paul.

She giggled complacently. 'Do you think she's more sexy than me?'

'Yes.'

He went to the drinks tray and poured them both a whisky. He needed a change of subject. She had delicate little feet, Paul noticed, which was unusual in a woman. And she wriggled a lot. The ever-incipient boredom of the young, which tied in with the way she fidgeted with her long blonde hair.

'Would you like to make love to me?'

Paul smiled. 'I'm in love with my wife.'

'What a bore.'

It was gone midnight and the bottle of whisky was half-empty when they all went to bed. Jennie protested she was afraid, insisted that Paul leave the bedroom door open, and appeared likely to burst into tears. But eventually they despatched her, and two minutes later they could hear her breathing deeply.

Steve lay on her side and pretended to go straight to sleep. Paul prodded her and tried to say friendly things about how tiresome young girls can be, and surely you weren't like that at nineteen.

'If she's still here tomorrow,' said Steve, 'I'll murder her myself.'

Paul wondered why she was being so unsympathetic to the poor girl. It wasn't like Steve to be vindictive. Jennie was wild and she played with people's lives, but she was engaging. Paul listened to the girl's steady breathing in the next room. He hoped nobody would kill her.

Tracy Leonard went into the church by herself. A single bell was tolling, calling the faithful of Melford Cross to worship. About fifty people were trailing across the green. Paul Temple locked the door of his Jaguar and joined the congregation. He took a hymn book from the verger as he entered the church, murmured: 'Good morning,' and sat in the pew beside Tracy Leonard. The organist was doodling a tuneless variation on a theme by Bach.

'Is this a pleasant coincidence?' Tracy Leonard whispered when she realised who was sitting next to her.

'Very pleasant,' Paul whispered.

Her scent contrasted nicely with the dust and leather smell of the church. She looked serenely poised in the grey two piece. Paul wondered again why Alfred Kelby had let her go in favour of Jennie Mortimer.

Paul had found himself immensely relieved as he left home. He hadn't realised what a strain the girl's presence imposed on them all. She was enjoying her role in the centre of a murder case. Tracy Leonard was more classically English.

'Why have you come here?' she asked.

'I wanted to see you. Perhaps we could have a talk when morning service is finished. On our way up to the house.'

She agreed. 'But I've an awful lot to do. The police are still disrupting us with their questions. I'd like to be back as soon as possible.'

The choir and vicar were moving up the aisle. The service was beginning. Paul relaxed for an hour to enjoy religion in the simple community. He appreciated Christianity with fields and animals and the wind whistling outside the church, where the changing seasons affected one's life and men worked to produce a visible necessity for their own lives. And the congregation made a joyfully restrained English noise.

The choir was better if you closed your eyes. They sounded enthusiastic, unsubtle and happy. They looked like the local schoolmaster, a garage mechanic, a few farm labourers and a reluctant rabble of schoolboys. Paul was oddly moved by the soloist, a fleshly man of fifty with an unhealthy face and a beautiful tenor voice. His voice soared to the beams of the church when he sang, clutching his stomach and looking absurdly pleased with himself. He was the kind of man who came into his own each Sunday, when his friends stopped laughing and the village listened to him in awe.

It was sad, Paul thought, that the vicar didn't realise the importance of his rural authenticity. He tried to relate God and his congregation to the big wide world, and so the mood was dispelled. He preached a sermon on the commandment 'Thou shall not kill', with exemplification from that morning's newspaper coverage of the Kelby story. The vicar was uncompromisingly against murder. Paul wondered as the service ended and the flock moved slowly out into the midday drizzle how may people the vicar thought he had saved from life imprisonment and damnation.

'Why on earth did you come here?' Tracy asked. 'We could perfectly well have talked at the house.'

'I wanted to talk to you away from the others.'

'The others?' she repeated in surprise.

'Mr Ashwood, Ronnie Kelby, the police, anyone else who might be around.'

She seemed about to say something, but she changed her mind and led the way to the gate. Paul fell into step beside her. She refused his offer of a lift in the dry Jaguar. She always walked to church and back, every Sunday. Hers was an ordered life.

'What happened last night, Mr Temple?' she asked after a moment. 'Why was Gladys murdered?'

'Because she knew who killed Alfred Kelby.'

Tracy walked on in silence. There were flowers in the hedgerow already, but Paul didn't know what they were. Small white flowers, probably weeds, and the fields looked very green in the slight rain. He resented the way London prevented him from knowing the time of the year. It was nearly three months since they had stayed at the cottage. He and Steve had spent Christmas there.

'Who did kill him, Mr Temple?' she asked tensely.

'The same person who killed Gladys,' he said noncommittally. 'Miss Leonard, after we found Kelby's body I talked to Leo Ashwood and his wife in the kitchen.'

'I know,' she said impatiently, 'I was there.'

'You weren't in the kitchen. Mrs Ashwood said she had to go into the village because she had forgotten something.'

'That's right. A suit of Mr Kelby's. She'd sent it to the cleaners. People worry about irrational things in moments of crisis.'

'Did she return to the village?'

'Yes,' said Tracy. She glanced at him sardonically. 'Mr Reed gave her a lift.' She clearly regarded the subject as irrelevant, but she tried to be helpful. 'Mr Reed called round just as you left. He'd heard about the murder and of course he was very upset. He embarrassed everyone by apologising about the diary and explaining that he had never imagined it would lead to this. I just had to get rid of him.'

Paul grinned. It was a scene he could imagine only too clearly.

'So I asked him to give Gladys a lift into the village. That got rid of both of them.'

'How did Gladys get back?' Paul asked.

'Her husband picked her up later.' She faltered in her stride and turned to Paul. 'Incidentally, Mr Reed telephoned me yesterday afternoon. He wants to talk to me about Mr Kelby's will. Apparently he and I are the executors.'

'You sound a little surprised,' said Paul. 'Didn't you know Mr Kelby had appointed you an executor?'

'No, I didn't.' She continued up the hill again. 'Well, I suppose I did. He said something about it ages ago. But he was always changing his mind about wills and that sort of thing. He probably imagined that every change in his will gave him a new lease of life. He was very superstitious. He didn't like to think that his death had been settled.'

When they reached the top of the hill Paul looked back at the village. It was a village like most others, but the design had never been improved on. He liked it.

'Look, Mr Temple, I don't want to be rude. But you still haven't told me what you want.'

'Eh? No, that's true. I haven't.' Paul smiled and turned away from the view. The road narrowed now towards Melford House. 'Last night I stuck my neck out and told Inspector Vosper I could solve this case. I told him I could solve it within twenty-four hours, provided two people were willing to help me.' He took her arm. 'I was referring to you, Miss Leonard. You and a man called Arthur Grover.'

'I've never heard of Arthur Grover.'

123

Paul laughed. 'I don't expect you have.'

'And I can't imagine how I would be able to help you.'

'I want you to go to the cinema,' he said enigmatically. He ignored her look of astonishment. 'I see they're showing *Vivre pour Vivre* at the local cinema. It's an excellent film. I've seen it twice.'

'Couldn't I go and see *The Seventh Seal* again in Oxford?' she asked.

'Good idea! You go and see *The Seventh Seal*. Go tonight.' He kissed her on the cheek and left her wondering which of them was mad.

Steve had finished her record sleeve. She was in the mood to be taken out and pampered. She had proved once again that she could be independent, she could be a success in her own right as a designer, so she was submissive and happy. She sat in the passenger seat of the Jaguar and watched the lights of Soho flash gaudily by.

'You'll have to spend the day in Melford Cross again, darling,' she said mischievously. 'Jeremy has given me a series of book jackets to design; he had some trouble with the girl who was doing them. I've had a very productive day.'

Paul was silent for a moment. He decided not to rise to her bait. 'I didn't spend the whole day in Melford Cross. I was back in town by two o'clock. Had lunch with Scott.'

'Oh.' She wondered why Paul was looking so earnest. 'Did he think your idea for the new novel was pompous?'

'No, he thought it sounded fine. Suggested I set it in a circus, with alcoholic midgets and a fat lady hooked on heroin. The victim should be fired from a cannon into the lions' cage because he was having an affair with a girl on the trapeze.'

'How do you make love on a trapeze?' Steve asked.

'It's difficult. That's how the husband finds out.'

Steve laughed. 'So you didn't discuss your novel with Scott. What did you talk about?'

'Alfred Kelby.'

They parked in a street behind the Casino Club and walked back. Steve was elegantly feminine in a red lace trouser suit. Paul had chosen it as a present. She wasn't quite sure about Paul's taste, but this evening she was pleased to be wearing it.

'Why the Casino Club in particular?' Steve asked him.

'It's owned by Arthur Grover and Neville Delamore.'

She stopped in the entrance and turned to Paul. 'You mean we're here on business? I thought we were having an evening out! Just you dare spoil it, Paul, that's all!'

A man in an admiral's uniform saluted them and swung the swing doors to spin them into the club. He said: 'Good evening, sir. Madam.' The foyer was crowded with premiere people, mink ladies and mark ten men, rich people with money to lose on the top floor. A notice on the wall said: 'Please Don't Touch the Pussy Cats.'

'They say there's only one original idea each century,' Paul murmured. The female staff were scantily costumed as cats. 'This idea was introduced into gambling back in San Francisco in 1849.'

'Don't pretend to get historical,' said Steve, 'just keep your attention under control.'

'It's helpful to distinguish the staff from the customers.'

The staff had long feline tails swinging from hairless pink buttocks, while the customers wore long dresses or dark trousers; the customers had hair or pink heads whereas the staff had fur and pointed ears; the staff used eye make-up to resemble demons of the Nile. The customers wore jackets or rather ample corsets while the staff wore inadequate cat fur cups.

'I thought this was *my* evening out?' said Steve. 'Why should *I* want to stare at all this female flesh?'

'We're mixing our pleasure with business, I'm afraid.'

Paul took her arm and guided her gently through the crush into the cocktail bar. It was a large bar designed as a roulette table. There was a Pussy Cat behind the bar.

'Good evening. My name is Temple. Mr Grover is expecting me.'

'Yes, of course sir,' she said with a smile. 'I'll let Mr Grover know you're here.' She went to the telephone at the back of the bar.

Paul said: 'You remember what Arthur Grover told me about his telephone call to Ronnie Kelby on the day the old boy disappeared?'

'Yes,' said Steve. She was watching a group of men who had arrived in a party with their secretaries. A convention of Midland industrialists living it up, she decided. They obviously had tabby cats and skinny wives back home in the Midlands. Their heads rotated hypnotically as each Pussy Cat passed.

'Well, he's making another phone call tonight.'

'Another call?' Steve looked at him for a moment. 'Why?'

'Because I've asked him to.'

Before Paul could explain Arthur Grover had arrived, waving his cigar and calling good evenings in all directions. He was wearing a dinner jacket that fitted him, Paul noticed, without any ugly bulges under the arm.

'Good evening, Mrs Temple. What would you like to drink? A dry martini?' He flicked his fingers at the girl behind the bar. 'Bunty mixes the best cocktails in London.'

Steve nodded approvingly.

'I gather you're helping my husband—'

126

'Yes, isn't that generous of me?' His friendly clubman manner didn't change as he continued: 'An American club owner in London to stay in business has to help all kinds of people. But I keep a list of them.' He laughed good-naturedly. 'If I ever see your husband down on the floor I'll kick his head in.'

Paul laughed. The previous telephone call had been made on Monday at a quarter to nine so they stayed in the bar exchanging pleasantries. Then at a quarter to nine they went through into Grover's office. As he passed the Pussy Cat working the lift Grover slapped her bottom loudly. The notice on the wall did not apply to him. He was still chuckling and rubbing his hands as he sat at his desk.

'Of course, on Monday I used a public call box,' he said as he picked up the phone and dialled. 'There's always the risk of a call being traced.' He flashed his teeth at Steve. 'Why don't you sit down, Mrs Temple?'

'Thank you.' Steve sat on a leather sofa and watched the man enjoying his own performance. She couldn't quite make out whether his amiability was sinister or his menace an illusion.

Paul heard the voice on the other end of the line as Grover said: 'Good evening. I've spoken to you once before, Mr Kelby, on the night your father disappeared. The night you killed him and took the body to Galloway Farm.' He nodded to Paul, confirming that he was speaking to the same man as before.

'I'm Arthur Grover, and you know perfectly well what I'm talking about! Your father was alive when we left him in the gardener's shed – he was alive when you found him.' There was a long pause. Paul wondered whether the person at the other end of the line had hung up. Suddenly Grover winked. 'Yes, Mr Kelby, of course I can prove it! I have a photograph of you carrying the body out of the shed.'

The man on the other end began talking quickly and excitedly. Grover gave Paul the thumbs up sign. The trick had worked.

'Come along, Steve, let's go and enjoy that meal.'

They left the office and went downstairs to the dining room.

'That was hardly a conclusive phone call,' Steve said. 'What's going to happen now?'

'Grover is arranging to meet the man who killed Alfred Kelby. To hand over the photographs.'

She smiled knowingly. 'But instead of Grover you'll keep the appointment?'

'That's right, Steve. Tomorrow morning at Marlow. Eleven o'clock.'

Steve sat nervously at the table and glanced at the menu. 'Couldn't we eat at a restaurant where the waiters are masculine and dressed as all-in wrestlers?' she sighed. 'From now on the evening out belongs to me.'

It was one o'clock when they got back home, but there were a surprising number of people about. There were two police cars in the mews and an ambulance arrived as Paul was getting out of the car. The others seemed to be passers-by with nothing better to do at night than watch a girl lying dead on the pavement.

'Oh God,' Paul muttered. 'He's got Jennie!'

She was wearing the outfit she had worn the previous night, and in the sulphur light from the street lamps her body could be seen twisted and smashed through the nylon. The huge puddle of blood was black in the light. She looked, Paul thought bitterly, like a child's broken doll.

Paul Temple and the Kelby Affair

Kate Balfour was talking to the police, telling them she had been with the girl all evening until at midnight she had popped home to fetch her sleeping things. 'I was only gone fifteen minutes . . .'

Paul knelt beside the girl and touched her cold face. She had fallen the fifty feet from the guest room window. He glanced up. It was meant to look like suicide.

'Poor girl,' Steve said quietly. 'She was so innocent really. I almost got to like her.'

129

Chapter 14

PAUL TEMPLE leaned over the parapet and looked down into the murky water. It was a fine morning and the sun was shining across the Thames; but the water was brown. Paul gestured to the police launch below. A uniformed sergeant and two plain-clothes men were ready. Paul glanced at his watch. Ten minutes to eleven.

Eight boys came rowing round the river bend. They were being yelled at through a megaphone: 'in-out-in-out, Bunter, in-out,' by an insane schoolmaster riding along the towpath on a bicycle. Paul watched in fascination to see whether the schoolmaster would ride into the river, but he didn't. He whisked up onto the bridge, rode past Paul and down onto the towpath on the opposite bank. 'In-out-in-out.'

Paul wondered uneasily which direction the killer would come from. It would be unthinkable, he thought ironically, to be killed without ever knowing it. He walked to the south end of the bridge and stared down the road from Henley. Of course, the killer might have been waiting the past two hours in the hotel by the river. The Compleat Angler. That would be the wisest place, to ensure that no ambush was set up. Paul strolled back to the north side. A Ford Zephyr police car was parked in the private entrance to a boatyard a few yards downstream. Then the clock struck eleven.

He had never established whether Gladys had been stabbed in the back, or whether the knife had been thrown by an expert at twenty yards. Paul braced his shoulders and turned round. The protection seemed an awful long way away. He felt rather conspicuous alone on the bridge.

A Rover 2000 was coming along the road from Henley. When it reached The Compleat Angler it turned off into the car park. Paul waited, and a few moments later Scott Reed came from the car park. He was scurrying towards the bridge like a nervous crab. The police had not moved.

Suddenly Scott Reed saw Paul on the bridge. His hand twitched involuntarily in the beginnings of a wave, then he stopped. He glanced backwards and forwards before hurrying down the steps to the towpath.

'Scott!' Paul shouted.

Paul ran to the stairs and called down to the publisher.

'Scott! What the hell are you doing here?'

Scott came up the stairs as four policemen converged on him from the nearby boathouse and the hotel. He smiled ingratiatingly.

'Oh, hello, Paul. I just came to see—'

'You damned fool,' Paul snapped. 'Don't you realise that you've upset the whole operation?'

'I was worried after what you told me yesterday. I just had to come—'

'Temple, look out!' someone shouted.

Paul swung round in time to see a man racing towards him from the opposite end of the bridge. Two more policemen were pursuing Leo Ashwood in Paul's direction. Leo stopped and drew a gun from his pocket. He fired a couple of shots, one at Paul and the second behind him at the police. When Paul peered cautiously round the side of the stone stairs a policeman was lying in a pool of blood, and Leo Ashwood was standing on the parapet. Nothing seemed to be happening.

'Leo,' Paul called, 'don't be silly. You're making things worse.'

'I'll shoot! Leave me alone!'

The stolid manservant was flourishing his gun with a wildness entirely due to panic. Paul hoped that the desperation would make his aim inaccurate.

'You can't escape,' Paul called. 'So let's be sensible. I'll come and collect the gun from you, and then the police will look after you. All right? I'm coming out!'

Paul stepped onto the bridge. He walked slowly along the pavement towards the centre. He felt extraordinarily relaxed, interested to find himself behaving like this and coldly rational about the even money that Leo might shoot. He felt slightly sorry for Leo. The man was terrified and trapped.

'I'll shoot,' Leo shouted. 'Don't think I won't kill you! You tricked me with that telephone call! Keep away, you bastard! You tricked me!'

Paul continued his walk towards him. He thought disinterestedly that Leo was talking in clichés. People under stress always fall back on clichés. Paul decided that if he lived to write his serious study of murder he would have to remember that. No elegant dialogue during the death throes. Whilst he was thinking this he was simultaneously aware of a car moving behind him. The fools, he thought to himself, they'll ruin everything!

'I'll shoot,' Leo shouted, a pleading tone adding to his desperation. 'Don't think I won't. I'll shoot!'

The Ford Zephyr had roared onto the bridge and it screeched to a halt beside the shot policeman. Its four doors flew open and three uniformed policemen sprang into the open. The fourth door had been opened by Charlie Vosper, but he didn't offer himself as a target. He waited until Leo had fired two more shots before emerging.

Leo was as surprised at the explosion of the gun as the policeman whose arm was splintered by a bullet. He staggered sideways and lost his balance. Paul ran forward to grab his legs, but Leo was waving his arms about as he toppled from the bridge. The gun went off again, harmlessly into the stonework of the bridge, while Paul tried to hang on to the ankle. Charlie Vosper grabbed the other leg, but Leo was too heavy. He fell with a scream into the river below.

'You're a bloody hero, aren't you?' Vosper snarled.

'It would have worked,' Paul said calmly.

Leo was swimming against the current now, swimming towards the bank as the police launch roared into action. It swung out into the centre of the river and headed for the same spot on the bank. But Leo was clearly not a strong swimmer and his clothes were hindering him. He disappeared underwater once, then reappeared splashing and spluttering. The police launch changed course and went straight for him.

'In-out-in-out! Come along there, Bunter, pull your weight. In-out!'

The insane schoolmaster whisked across the bridge, skidded past the shot policeman, and came to a halt in a heap by the Ford Zephyr. His megaphone landed at Paul's feet.

The eight schoolboys lost their rhythm and drifted chaotically into the path of the police launch. The sixteen oars began clicking against each other and the boat swung sideways onto the current before tipping onto its side.

Leo screamed for help as he came up for the second time. But the police launch had hit the rowing boat. An awful crack of splintering wood was followed by schoolboy shouts of dismay. While the three policemen concentrated on rescuing the boys Leo Ashwood drowned.

Chapter 15

STEVE put the little black number back into the wardrobe as she heard the door open downstairs. He was back. Steve peered over the balcony to watch him arrive in the living room. She didn't dare move or call out, not until she had seen . . . It was a feeling she had experienced before and it only lasted for a few seconds. A feeling of dread.

'Steve! It's me!' Paul shouted cheerfully.

'Hi.' She waved over the balcony and then came down the spiral staircase. 'You sound as if it all went well.' She was the sensible, coolly poised wife again, apart from the smile that extended almost into a grin.

'It didn't go too well,' he said happily. 'It's always bad when a man is dragged off by the currents and drowned. And a couple of policemen received minor injuries. The best we can say is that events have reached a formally predetermined conclusion. The pattern has been completed.'

'You pompous idiot,' Steve laughed.

'All right, so who's a superstitious ninny?' he teased. 'You were invoking the spirits over that black dress again, weren't you?'

She hung her head. 'It worked,' she murmured.

He kissed her lightly on top of the head.

'I'm always glad when a case is over,' he admitted. 'I'll
be able to do some work now. At nine o'clock tomorrow
morning I'll be starting work, office hours, nine to five. I'm
looking forward to the dull routine again.' He sat at the huge
desk and patted the typewriter like an old friend. 'Nothing
but boredom for the next few weeks, I'm pleased to say.'
He swung round on the swivel chair. 'Speaking of boredom,
Scott Reed invited us down to Hambledon for dinner tonight.'

'Oh no,' said Steve. 'Do we have to?'

'No, of course not.' Paul smiled reassuringly. 'I told him
we'd go out to that pub in Hindhead for supper.'

'Wait a minute,' she began cautiously. 'Won't that be work
again? You'll be researching into that heavyweight study of
murder!' She flounced into the kitchen. 'When am I going
to be given a treat because you want to give me a treat? I
refuse to come!'

The restaurant behind the pub overlooked the Devil's
Punchbowl, a massive dip in the Surrey downs lined with trees
and bracken on every side. The main road south wound partly
along the top of the rim in a perilous arc, and as darkness
fell the bowl itself was lost in inky nothing and the stream
of headlamps cutting through the night became yellow and
mysterious. Paul felt as if they were dining on the edge of the
world, watching a Gadarene stampede of cars in the distance.

'You're not very good company, darling,' Steve intruded
into his thoughts.

'Eh? No, I'm sorry. I was thinking about the Kelby affair.
It was boorish of me.' He tucked into the vegetable soup
and said something about soup like they used to make soup.

'I know how you must feel,' Scott's wife said sympatheti-
cally. 'I should think the end of a murder case must leave
one very sad, like having made love in the afternoon.'

Paul smiled. 'Yes, it is something like that.' He began talking about the case before Scott Reed could challenge his wife about her analogy. He explained about the trap they had set to catch Leo.

'I had to tell Scott what I was doing,' he explained, 'because I needed the information about Kelby's will. And the stubborn devil refused to give it to me unless I took him into my confidence.' Scott was smiling and sitting there with his slimly dignified wife as if the world began and ended with first editions of significant modern novels. He didn't want to know when she last made love in the afternoon. 'Kelby was about to make a new will in favour of his son.'

'I suppose Leo Ashwood knew that,' said Steve.

'Precisely. He also knew that the current will was very much in his favour. Until Ronnie came home like a prodigal son Leo stood to inherit nearly everything. So he must have been pretty furious. Just waiting, in fact, for an opportunity such as Arthur Grover gave him.'

'He could,' Mrs Reed suggested bloodthirstily, 'have simply bumped Kelby off in the night. Any night.'

'Perhaps he meant to. But when Grover telephoned during the evening it was a marvellous opportunity. Ronnie was out with Tracy Leonard, remember, they were searching for Kelby. So the moment Grover said he had information—'

'Leo,' Steve interrupted, 'pretended he was Ronnie Kelby.'

'Right. He realised that his murder was ready and waiting to be committed. All Leo had to do was go into the gardener's shed and strangle Alfred Kelby. Then he took the body across to Galloway Farm.'

'In order to throw suspicion on Ted Mortimer.'

'Yes.' Paul tasted his ham and found it satisfactory. He ate a small piece of pineapple. 'Ted Mortimer was a well-known enemy of nearly everybody in Melford Cross. Still is, I suppose, poor devil.'

They continued eating in silence. Paul was wondering whether he could have saved the life of Jennie Mortimer.

'I suppose,' Steve said brightly, 'that as soon as Arthur Grover rang up Melford House and said that he had some photographs of Leo disposing of the body, he knew who had taken the photographs. Jennie Mortimer's life wasn't worth living.'

'Do you think so?' Paul asked. He filled his glass with more wine. 'But how could she have taken the photographs?'

'Well,' she laughed, 'I know there weren't any photographs. But if Jennie had been meeting Kelby that night—'

'She hadn't been!' Paul ate in silence for a full two minutes. He wished the tone of the conversation wasn't so resolutely cheerful. He wished they didn't expect him to be good company. They were casting accusing glances in his direction. 'All right,' he said, 'Jennie did see Kelby in answer to that letter we found. She saw him at ten o'clock at their usual meeting place. But she saw him two weeks before he died.'

Steve squeezed his leg in sympathy under the table. She shrugged helplessly, as if she knew what it was like. It was a nice gesture, and Paul smiled gratefully.

'What about that shoe I was left with?' Scott Reed asked insensitively. 'Did Leo used to inherit Kelby's old clothes?'

'Well done, Scott!' Paul genuinely laughed at the man's enthusiasm to know all the trivial details. 'Leo was wearing a pair of shoes he'd been given by Kelby. And poor Gladys! She came to see me because she knew her husband was the killer. When he had brought her back from the Melford Cross dry cleaners he had talked of Kelby being *strangled*, not just murdered. That was how she knew, although I expect she was beginning to guess the truth about Leo the day before she came to see me.'

'She must have guessed,' Steve agreed, convinced of the power of feminine intuition. 'But how did you manage to get Ronnie out of the house so that Leo would take Grover's second phone call?'

'That wasn't easy. But I caught Tracy Leonard in a Christian frame of mind, and I persuaded her to take Ronnie to the cinema.' He smiled to himself and then gestured to the wine waiter. 'It wasn't easy. She hates the sight of Ronnie, and he's been making passes at her for weeks. I hope they won't blame me if they eventually marry and live unhappily ever after.'

He ordered another bottle of wine. It was a pleasantly euphoric evening, the ham and the wine and the open range coal fire lulled them comfortably into a mood of pastoral credulity. After an hour or so the real world became less real and guilt lost its edge of pain. Paul began telling them about the sailor who was hanged beside the pub so many years ago. It was a gothic, mythic world beyond the window, a world of good and evil and of cars hurtling towards the cliff of destruction, a country scene where devils drank punch and night was filled with electric storms.

'Send for the landlord,' said Paul. 'He'll know about the local folklore. Ask him to join us for the brandy.'

Steve smiled, resigned herself to doing the driving back to London, and asked the landlord to join them. 'My husband is researching a book on gratuitous death,' she explained. The landlord had a morbid turn of mind as well. He joined them.

'Local legend has it,' he told Paul Temple, 'that it was a ritual murder. Some secret cult being practised down there in the clearing.' He was a bluff military type, a retired major, and the folklore would not disturb his sleep.

'Why was it never solved?' Paul asked him.

'I don't know. The police were out of their depth. We had an exactly similar murder here last month, and they aren't making any progress with that. A good job it doesn't happen very often.'

'Exactly similar?'

Paul and the landlord became lost in conversation. Steve recognised the eager interest her husband was showing. So much for the life of boredom they had been looking forward to. She turned to Scott Reed and his wife and began talking of plays they had seen and books they had read and whether Scott Reed's son would become a publisher. She wished they had stayed at home that evening.

In her experience Paul was less sad when they made love in the afternoon.